FROM THE
NANCY DREW FILES

THE CASE: Nancy must find Jack Broughton's killer before the case ruins Carson Drew's reputation.

CONTACT: Broughton worked for Nancy's father, and his body was found at the law firm.

SUSPECTS: Kyle Donovan—*Bess's new boyfriend wants to go to law school, a plan Broughton threatened to destroy.*

Al Fortunato—*A junkyard dealer and another of Broughton's victims, he has the temper of a junkyard dog.*

Carson Drew—*Can the unthinkable be true? The police have already searched his office and home, refusing to cross him off the list of suspects.*

COMPLICATIONS: Bess's boyfriend? Her own father? How can Nancy conduct a thorough, unbiased investigation when the case hits so close to home?.

Books in The Nancy Drew Files® Series

The Nancy Drew Files™

Case 88

False Pretenses
Carolyn Keene

AN ARCHWAY
Published
New York   London

AN ARCHWAY PAPERBACK *Original*

An Archway Paperback published by
POCKET BOOKS, a division of Simon & Schuster Inc.
1230 Avenue of the Americas, New York, NY 10020

Copyright © 1993 by Simon & Schuster Inc.
Produced by Mega-Books of New York, Inc.

ISBN: 0-671-79480-9

First Archway Paperback printing October 1993

10 9 8 7 6 5 4 3 2 1

NANCY DREW, AN ARCHWAY PAPERBACK and colophon are registered trademarks of Simon & Schuster Inc.

THE NANCY DREW FILES is a trademark of Simon & Schuster Inc.

Cover art by Tricia Zimic

Printed in the U.S.A.

IL 6+

False Pretenses

Chapter

One

N ANCY DREW flipped through the dresses on the circular rack. The fashions that fall seemed to come in only two colors—brown or rust.

"Well, Nancy? What do you think?"

Nancy turned. Her friend Bess Marvin had just come out of the dressing room. She was standing in front of the three-panel mirror, frowning at the many reflections of herself in a dark plaid kilt and rust brown Shetland sweater. Her blond hair fell over one shoulder and her blue eyes sparkled, in spite of her thoughtful frown.

"It's not very radical, is it?" Bess added.

"I think the word for it is *classic*," Nancy replied with a laugh.

"You're right," Bess said. "But the next ques-

1

tion is, do you think Kyle will like it? This is a big date tonight, and I want to look just right."

Kyle Donovan was Bess's new boyfriend. Twenty-one and just out of college, he was working in the law firm of Nancy's dad, Carson Drew, while he saved his money to go to law school. Nancy had introduced the tall, good-looking newcomer to Bess.

"With a name like Donovan, he's bound to," Nancy pointed out. "Men wear kilts in Ireland, too, you know."

"Honestly, Nancy," Bess said. "I'm not buying it for *him* to wear! Maybe I should go for something a little more 'now.' Did you notice those leather jeans near the entrance? The ones with all the straps and buckles?"

Nancy decided that it was time to take a more active part in Bess's deliberations. "I noticed them," she admitted. "But frankly, Bess, they may be *now*, but they're not really *you*. Why not something like this?"

She reached into the rack next to her and pulled out a drop-waist dress in a floral print. Sighing, Bess took it and held it up to herself in front of the mirror. "I wish George hadn't gone out of town," she fretted. George Fayne was Bess's cousin and also Nancy's close friend. "She always knows what looks good on me."

Nancy studied Bess's face in the mirror and thought her friend looked troubled—about

2

something other than making a decision about what to buy.

"Bess?" she said. "Is something wrong? Do you want to talk about it?"

All at once Bess's eyes filled with tears.

"What is it?" Nancy demanded. "Something between you and Kyle? I thought you were getting along fantastically."

"We are," Bess replied. She paused to brush the tears from her cheeks. "At least, we were . . . I think. Oh, I don't know, Nancy. One of the things I like about Kyle is the way he always cheers me up. And when he gives me that funny, lopsided smile of his, my heart turns over. The past week he's been so strange, though. So moody and depressed. Sometimes when I talk to him, I have the feeling he's a thousand miles away and hasn't heard a word I've said."

"Ned gets that way at finals time," Nancy remarked. Ned Nickerson, her longtime boyfriend, was a student at Emerson College. "Maybe Kyle is worried about something. Isn't he planning to take the law boards to get into law school in a couple of months?"

Bess burst out, "That's just it! You know how going to law school is supposed to be the most important thing in his life? Well, now, all of a sudden, he's started talking about not going!"

"That *is* strange," Nancy said, shaking her head. "And you have no idea what started this?"

3

"He won't talk to me about it," Bess replied. "I've tried, but he just clams up."

She hesitated, then continued. "I was hoping you might be able to find out what's going on. Maybe something happened at his job—it's the only possibility I can think of. Do you think you could ask your father about it?"

Nancy frowned. "That's a little tricky, Bess. After all, Dad *is* Kyle's employer. Kyle might not appreciate my interfering. He might not appreciate *your* interfering, either."

"I know. I thought of that," Bess replied, staring down at the floor. "But if Kyle is in trouble, I want to help him."

Nancy took her arm and turned her in the direction of the dressing room. "Look, it's probably nothing," she said. "There's not much I can do now, anyway. My dad's out of town on an important case. He's due back tomorrow morning, but he said he was going straight to the office. I probably won't even see him until tomorrow evening."

"I understand," Bess said, downcast.

Nancy went on, "If Kyle still seems worried when you see him tonight, tell him how concerned you are and ask him to let you help."

"Tonight!" Bess yelped. "It's practically tonight already, and I still don't have anything to wear. Nancy, help!"

Laughing, Nancy pointed to the dress Bess was

still holding. "Try that on," she advised. "And if you don't like it, go home and look through your closet again. I know you'll find something. And remember—it's *you* Kyle wants to go out with, not your clothes!"

After Nancy had dinner alone with Hannah Gruen, the Drews' housekeeper, she carried their dishes to the kitchen. She was trying to convince Hannah to let her do the washing up when the phone rang. Nancy ran for it, hoping to hear her father's voice.

"Nancy, it's me," Bess said in a soft voice.

Alarmed by her tone, Nancy demanded, "Bess, is something wrong?"

"What could possibly be wrong?" Bess replied drearily. "What do I care if my date just called to say that he has to work late and what about going out next week? Am I bothered? Am I blue?"

"Yes, and yes," Nancy said, her mind racing. She had planned on calling Ned and then curling up with a murder mystery. That could wait now. Bess needed her.

"Bess?" she continued. "I've got an idea. Why don't I pick up a movie and some popcorn and come over to your place? Have you seen *Singin' in the Rain?*"

"Of course I have," Bess said indignantly. "But I'd love to see it again." She started humming the title song.

"Okay. I'll see you in a little while," Nancy concluded.

Half an hour later she began to think that it wasn't her day to be a Good Samaritan. The convenience store nearest her house was out of microwave popcorn, and when she asked Jerry, the manager of the video store, for *Singin' in the Rain,* he shook his head and said, "Sorry, Nancy. A guy checked out our only copy a couple hours ago. Our branch downtown might have it, though. You want me to see?"

"Thanks, I'd appreciate it." As Jerry reached for the phone, Nancy wondered if Bess would be just as happy with another musical, such as *An American in Paris* or *Brigadoon.* No, she had had one big disappointment already that evening. There was no point in piling on another, no matter how minor.

"They're holding it for you," Jerry announced, hanging up the phone. "Do you know how to find our downtown store?"

"I've passed it a hundred times. It's right across from my father's office," Nancy assured him.

"Okay, then. Have a nice evening."

As she drove downtown, Nancy found herself wondering about Kyle. She knew that paralegals like Kyle often had to work late. Yet as far as she knew, the only urgent case her dad's firm was involved in was the one that had taken him out of town. Nancy couldn't imagine what last-minute task Kyle would be working on for that case.

As she swung the blue Mustang into Judiciary Square, her eye automatically traveled to the tallest building on the block and up to the floor where her father's offices were. Some of the windows were lit, which was no surprise. People who worked late didn't do it in the dark.

Her mind flashed back to her earlier conversation with Bess. Just what could be bothering Kyle? Something about the way he was being treated at work? Was someone picking on him or dealing with him unfairly? If so, Nancy might be able to drop a hint to her father and get the situation straightened out. It wouldn't hurt to try, she decided.

She found a spot across the street from the office building and parked the Mustang. As she locked the door, she noticed that the streets were practically empty, even though it wasn't yet seven. The video store was lit, as was the coffee shop back the other way, but all the other shops were dark.

"I bet you're here for *Singin' in the Rain,*" the clerk said when she walked into the store. "It's all ready for you."

Nancy paid the fee and took the cassette box. As she returned to her car, she glanced up at the windows of her father's offices again. What if she dropped by on some invented errand and accidentally ran into Kyle? Maybe she could manage to find out what was troubling him without giving him the impression that she was meddling. It was worth a try.

She crossed the street and entered the building. As she started toward the bank of elevators, an older man in a blue uniform appeared from the back of the lobby.

"Just a moment, miss," he called. "You'll have to sign in."

He walked over to a small desk against the side wall, next to the building directory, and took a dog-eared notebook and pencil from the drawer.

"You're Mr. Drew's daughter, aren't you?" he asked as he opened the notebook to the first blank page and handed it to her. "I've seen you with him. He's a real gentleman, your dad."

Nancy blushed with pleasure. "Thank you," she replied. She signed her name on the top line and added the floor of her father's offices, then glanced at her watch.

"It's just seven," the guard said. "That's when we start asking people to sign in. You're my first customer of the day."

"Thanks," Nancy murmured again, and wrote in the time. "See you later."

The elevator went nonstop to the firm's floor. The highly polished wooden double doors that led into Carson Drew's offices were directly across the hall from the elevators. Nancy frowned. Ordinarily, the doors were locked after business hours, and late visitors had to ring a bell and wait to be let in. Now, though, the left-hand door was slightly ajar. She pushed it open and stepped inside.

The wood-paneled reception area was empty. A brass lamp on the mahogany corner table cast a soft glow over the two leather-upholstered armchairs that flanked it. Nancy breathed in deeply. She always loved the air in her dad's office, heady with the tang of lemon-oil furniture polish and the musty scent of old leather-bound law books.

The firm took up most of the floor. Down a short hall to the left were her father's office and the conference room. The desk just outside them belonged to Ms. Hanson, Carson Drew's secretary. A long corridor to the right led to the firm's library and a series of offices occupied by associates and paralegals.

Nancy went to the head of the right-hand corridor. "Hello?" she called. "Is anybody here? It's me, Nancy Drew."

No one answered, but she thought she heard a faint rustling sound somewhere down the hall. She stood very still, held her breath, and listened hard. The sound was not repeated.

Nancy's heart started to pound. If the offices were empty, someone had been terribly negligent in leaving the outer door open and the lights on. And if someone were here, he obviously had a reason to keep his presence secret. Either way, it meant trouble—and possibly danger.

Stealthily, she started down the hallway. Most of the offices that lined it were dark, but at the end light spilled out from the open door to the law library. She tiptoed up to it and walked into the room, then choked back a gasp of horror.

A man in dark trousers and a shirt and sweater was sprawled facedown across the long oak table in the center of the room. Nancy couldn't see his face, but the unnatural angle of his head told her that he was almost certainly dead.

Chapter

Two

NANCY STEPPED OUT into the corridor and peered up and down. Back in the library she circled the body and bent over to study the face. She didn't recognize the man. A heavy law book was lying on the table. The murder weapon? That was one of the questions the police would have to answer. It was time to get them on the phone.

Making sure not to touch anything, Nancy stood up and carefully searched the room with her eyes only. All four walls were lined with tall oak bookcases filled with row after row of law books. Nancy noticed a gap in one of the rows, a little below shoulder height just to the right of the door. The volume on the desk appeared to be a part of that series.

Had the victim been working there? It didn't

seem so. Aside from the law book, the surface of the table was bare. No legal pads, no index cards, no pens or pencils and the overturned old-fashioned reading lamp on the table wasn't lit.

As she returned to the reception area, Nancy paused and listened at each of the office doors she passed. She didn't dare try the knobs. The killer might have left his prints on one of them—or on the telephone at the receptionist's desk. How was she going to call the police? She picked up the receiver with a tissue and used the eraser end of a pencil to punch in 911. Then she settled down in one of the leather chairs to wait.

It wasn't long before she heard the wail of sirens, then the whine of the elevator. The door-bell rang. She looked through the peephole and opened the door. Almost before she knew it, the reception area filled with uniformed offi-cers, plainclothes detectives, and a team of para-medics.

A tall, thin man with short black hair, a narrow mustache, and chestnut skin seemed to be in charge. Nancy didn't recognize him. Maybe he was a recent addition to the River Heights Police Department, she thought.

He came over to her. "Ms. Drew? I'm Detec-tive Washington. You put in the call about a killing here?"

"That's right," Nancy replied. "The victim's down the hall, in the law library. You can't miss it—the ceiling lights are on, and the door's open."

The paramedics, detectives, and one of the uniformed officers took off quickly in that direction. The second uniformed officer moved over to stand in front of the door to the elevators.

In a short time Detective Washington returned. He took a notebook from his hip pocket. "Would you mind telling me how you came to discover the body, Ms. Drew?"

"My father is Carson Drew, and this is his office," Nancy explained. "I came downtown to pick up a video. When I noticed the lights were on up here, I thought a friend of mine, Kyle Donovan, might be working late, so I came up to say hi. When I got upstairs, I found the front door open, which worried me, so I took a look around and found the man in the library."

"Did you see anyone else?"

Nancy shook her head. "No. But I didn't search, because I didn't want to ruin fingerprints by touching things."

The detective nodded. "Good thinking," he said. "Let's see—you arrived just after seven o'clock, is that right?"

"Why, yes," Nancy replied. "How—oh, of course, the sign-in sheet."

"And your call to the police department was logged in at seven twelve," Washington continued. "Twelve minutes seems a little long to find the body and call the police, doesn't it, Ms. Drew? Did you do anything else, anything you forgot to mention?"

Nancy gazed up toward the corner of the room. "I don't think so," she said. "Let me see—I chatted with the watchman for a minute or two after signing in. Then the elevator ride. Then I entered the office, looked around, tiptoed down to the library, and came back to call you. Twelve minutes doesn't sound about right for all that to you?"

"Hmm." Detective Washington seemed to be unhappy. He was opening his mouth to ask another question when the officer at the front door said, "Hey, where do you think you're going?"

Nancy turned. The officer was blocking the way of a cute guy with light brown hair and brown eyes. He was of medium height, with broad shoulders and a narrow waist, and looked to be in his early twenties. He wore jeans, a plaid sport shirt, and a leather jacket. Nancy had never seen him before.

"My name's David Megali. I'm a free-lance journalist," he told the officer. He took out his wallet and handed him some pieces of identification, which the officer passed to Detective Washington.

After scanning them and asking for his current address and phone number, he handed them back. Washington then motioned for the officer to let him in. "What brings you here, Mr. Megali?" he asked.

Megali frowned. "I could say I saw you and your team come in and decided to follow, in hopes of uncovering a story," he replied. Then he sighed. "But that wouldn't be true. The fact is, I have an appointment here. What's going on?"

"Oh? With whom?" Washington said, ignoring the man's question.

"I don't know," Megali said. Nancy thought he was beginning to sound frustrated. "I was following up on an anonymous call. Somebody left a message on my answering machine, promising to give me startling evidence."

"Evidence of what?" the detective demanded.

Megali hesitated, then said, "I'm looking into abuses suffered by elderly patients in nursing homes. Specifically, the embezzlement of funds held in trust for them. It's pretty shocking stuff, with millions of dollars at stake."

Nancy broke in. "You mean you came up here tonight on the basis of an anonymous phone call?"

"I had to," he replied, turning to her. "I've found that the hottest tips usually come from people who have good reason to keep their identities secret. Now what happened here, Detective?"

It was Washington's turn to hesitate. "An

apparent homicide," he finally said. He was about to add to that when his partner appeared in the doorway and beckoned to him. The two had a whispered conversation. Then the partner returned to the crime scene and Washington rejoined Nancy and David Megali.

"Does the name Jack Broughton mean anything to either of you?" he asked.

Megali shook his head. "Sorry, no."

"Why, yes," Nancy said. "My dad mentioned that name just a week or two ago. He was working here on some kind of short-term project—I don't remember what. Was he the victim?"

"It looks that way," Washington replied. "We located the jacket of his suit in a small office a couple of doors from the library. Ms. Drew, are you aware that there's a vault built into the library? The vault door is hidden by one of the bookshelves. We've called in an expert to examine it, but it appears to have been tampered with."

"Somebody broke into the firm's safe?" Nancy demanded. "That's awful!"

"We think someone may have *tried* to," the detective said, correcting her. "It may be that the victim had the bad luck to walk in on a burglary. The burglar might have tried to silence him and done too good a job. He'd have to have pretty strong nerves to go on trying to open the safe

16

after he'd committed a murder. Still, we need positive identification of the victim. We also need someone from the firm who's familiar with the contents of the vault to check it over. Is your father home? Maybe we can get him down here."

"No, he's not," Nancy replied. "He's been out of town the last couple of days. He's expected back tomorrow morning."

"I see," Detective Washington said. "Would you mind waiting here for a little while? I may have some other questions for you. You, too, Mr. Megali."

As he sat down with Nancy, David Megali said, "I've heard of you. You're earning yourself quite a reputation as a detective around this town. Have you ever thought of taking up investigative journalism? It has a lot in common with detective work."

"Really?" Nancy said, intrigued.

"Sure," David continued. "Take this case—I mean, I don't really buy this burglary business. I get an anonymous call offering me evidence of criminal activity, I arrive here and find that someone has been murdered. It's pretty obvious, isn't it? The victim must be the guy who was planning to give me the evidence. But he wasn't careful enough. Somebody found out what he was up to and killed him before he could pass on his information. It's the only explanation that makes sense."

17

THE NANCY DREW FILES

"Not quite," Nancy pointed out. "It could have been the killer who made the appointment with you, hoping that you'd show up in time to be the number one suspect. He couldn't have known that I'd get here before you."

David nodded and smiled wryly. "I can see why you have the reputation you do. I take it you don't have much faith in Detective Washington's burglary theory, either?"

"It raises a lot of unanswered questions," Nancy admitted. "For instance, how did the burglar get in? There's no sign of forced entry, or if there is, the police aren't telling us about it. And it's hard to imagine why a burglar would break in when somebody was still working in the office. Why not wait until the place was empty?"

"Do you have another theory?" David asked.

"Not so far," she hedged. "But I do think this crime calls for a more thorough investigation."

"Just what I was thinking!" he exclaimed. Lowering his voice, he added, "And my other thought was that this killing may very well be linked to the story I'm working on. What do you say we join forces? I think we would complement each other very well."

Nancy's thoughts raced. If David was what he seemed to be, his skills as a journalist could be useful to her investigation. If he *wasn't*—if he was somehow involved in the crime—working with him would give her a way of checking him out without arousing his suspicions.

"That sounds like a good idea," she said. Then, wondering if she had been a little too enthusiastic, she added, "We can try, anyway, and see how it works out. Who are you doing the story for?"

David named an important national magazine with a bureau in Chicago, then said, "Of course, I am doing the story on spec, which means I have no guarantee they'll take it when I'm done. It's the way things work—"

Detective Washington returned and cut David off. "I don't think we need to keep you two any longer tonight," he said. "But I'd appreciate it if you'd come down to headquarters tomorrow to give a formal statement."

His tone of voice made it clear that his request was actually an order.

"Certainly, Detective Washington," Nancy said. "What about locking up tonight? And what about tomorrow? Will my dad's office be able to open?"

"We should finish our crime-scene investigation before morning, and we'll get the security guard to lock up," he replied. "Oh—Mr. Megali? I tried your telephone number, and it's not working."

David looked startled. "It isn't? Let me see!" He glanced down at the detective's notebook and

19

gave an awkward laugh. "I'm sorry, officer," he said. "I told you five-five-six-five, and it's really five-*six*-six-five. I guess I haven't been in town long enough to have it down completely."

"I see. Thanks for the explanation." Washington made a note in his book. "That's all, then. I'll see you two tomorrow."

Downstairs, Nancy gave David her phone number and wrote his down. She noticed that this time he got it right. After agreeing to be in touch the next day, they separated. Nancy retrieved her car, remembered Bess, and drove straight to her house.

Bess was standing out on the porch beside the open front door before Nancy had switched off her engine.

"Where have you been?" she demanded as Nancy came up the walk. "I thought you were coming straight here. I've been so worried."

"It's a long story. I apologize for not remembering to call. Let's go inside and I'll tell you all about it," Nancy replied.

Once in the living room, Nancy told an openmouthed Bess about her eventful evening. When she finished, Bess said, "Nancy, how awful! You must be a complete wreck! But the thing I don't understand is, where was Kyle? Wasn't he supposed to be working late tonight? That's what he told me. I'm going to call him right now!"

There was no answer at Kyle's. "I guess he

changed his plans," Bess said a little shakily as she replaced the receiver. "Thank goodness—if he'd been there, *he* might have been murdered, too!"

Nancy nodded and put on a sympathetic expression. As she sat with Bess, watching the movie, she was paying more attention to some troubling questions than to the video. Where *had* Kyle been when the murder was committed? He was supposed to be at the office. Had he been? If so, he might have vital information that would help solve the crime. In that case, why hadn't he alerted the police about Broughton's death?

As Nancy drove home, she admitted to herself that there was one obvious answer to that question. She could barely bring herself to think about it, but trying to ignore it would not make it go away.

Kyle's actions made perfect sense—if he were the killer.

Chapter

Three

As NANCY TURNED into the driveway, she was surprised to see that her father's car was in the garage. She also noticed a light on in his study. Apparently, his out-of-town business hadn't taken as long as he expected.

Slowly she walked into the house. She hated being the bearer of bad news. The study door was ajar. Carson Drew was sitting at the desk with four or five thick files open in front of him and a yellow pad on his lap. He was chewing on the cap of his ballpoint pen.

Nancy tapped on the door. Her father raised his eyes and smiled. "Hi, Nan. I was wondering where you were."

"I wasn't expecting to see you till tomorrow. You came home early," she said, smiling back at him.

"There was a flight and my business was done, so I caught it."

As she walked into the room, Nancy noticed that his face was very drawn. "You look tired," she remarked. "Did you have a hard trip?"

"So-so," he replied. "Product liability cases are always complicated, and I have an important court date on this one tomorrow afternoon. I hope I get to bed sometime tonight, but it's starting to look doubtful."

Normally, Nancy would take this as a cue to say good night. Instead she pulled up a chair opposite him.

He raised an eyebrow in surprise. "Is something wrong?" he asked.

"Unfortunately, yes," Nancy said. "I was down at the office just now. There was some serious trouble there tonight."

"Trouble?" he repeated, frowning. "What sort of trouble?"

Nancy hesitated. "Well—I'm afraid one of your people, Jack Broughton, was killed. I discovered his body. The police think he must have interrupted a burglary."

"Broughton? Killed? That's terrible!" Carson exclaimed. He was silent for a moment, absorbing the news. Then he added, "But what were you doing there?"

Nancy hesitated. She couldn't tell her dad

anything less than the truth, she decided. "Bess mentioned that Kyle might be working late tonight," she said. "So when I saw the lights on, I dropped by to say hello."

Her father didn't seem to hear her. "Jack Broughton, dead . . ." he said in a distant voice. "What an awful, awful thing. He can't have been more than twenty-four or -five. I'll have to get in at the crack of dawn tomorrow. I don't want the others to hear about this from anyone but me. And I'll need to talk to the police tonight. I think I'll wait a minute, though."

"Yes," Nancy agreed. "Broughton just started to work for you, didn't he?"

"Hmm? Yes, that's right," Carson answered distractedly.

The crime had obviously hit him very hard, Nancy thought. She couldn't remember the last time he had seemed so preoccupied, so remote. His distress gave her an additional reason for wanting to solve this murder.

Carson made a steeple with his forefingers and touched them to the tip of his chin. "Broughton came to work for us just last month. He is—was, I should say—an interesting kid. He dropped out of law school after a couple of semesters but then made himself into something of an expert on computer filing systems for law firms. He worked for three or four well-known firms in different parts of the country, reorganizing and computerizing their files. I had hired him to come and do the same for me."

"How far did he get with his work with you?"

Carson sighed. "Not very far, I'm afraid. When he gave me a progress report last week he was still familiarizing himself with our old system. I doubt if he had time to do much more than that before tonight. In any case, none of this is relevant, considering that he was killed by an intruder."

After a moment Carson added, "I'm sorry, Nan. I need a little time to take this in." He bent his head down and pinched the bridge of his nose between his thumb and forefinger.

Nancy stood up. "I understand, Dad," she said. "It's a shame about Broughton. But at least I may be able to do something to help bring his killer to justice."

Carson raised his head quickly. "You intend to get involved in this case? We'd better have a serious talk about that," he said. "If anything happened to you . . ."

"It won't," she assured him. "This isn't the first time I've chased a murderer, you know. And besides, I'm already involved. I did find the body and report it to the police. I want to solve this crime before any rumors start that might damage your firm."

Her father nodded slowly. "I don't for a moment doubt your abilities as a detective. It's the risk that disturbs me."

"But, Dad, I've run risks before in other cases!"

"I know, and I dreaded every moment of them," he admitted. "Besides, this time it's me and my law practice that you're trying to help. That puts a responsibility on me beyond even my responsibility as your father."

Nancy knew that unless she insisted, she and her father were about to find themselves at a stalemate.

"I've got to work on this case," she said, drawing in a deep breath. "If I have your cooperation, the investigation will be a lot easier and a lot less risky. But risky or not, it's something I feel I have to do. Will you help me?"

He studied her for a long moment, then nodded his head. "All right," he said at last. "I'll do what I can. But I want you to promise that you'll be *very* careful."

"You have it," Nancy said simply.

"I want you to keep me informed at all times about what you've discovered and what you plan to do. Is that a deal?" he added.

Nancy blinked. Her father didn't usually act like a watchdog on her cases. Still, this one did concern his firm, so maybe he had a right to ask.

In the end she said, "Okay, Dad. I will. Good night."

"Good night, Nancy." As she left the room, he picked up the phone and started punching in his office number.

When Nancy came downstairs and into the kitchen the next morning, she spotted a cereal bowl and coffee cup in the drying rack by the sink. Her father was already up and gone, she realized. Hannah wasn't around, either. She found half a grapefruit in the refrigerator, poured herself a glass of milk, toasted a muffin, and sat down at the breakfast table. As she ate, she made notes about the case. Before leaving the house, she called Bess.

"Did you hear from Kyle last night after I left?" she asked.

"Not a word," Bess said. "Nancy, you don't think anything happened to him?"

"Don't be silly, of course not," Nancy replied. "Listen, I have to give a statement at police headquarters this morning, but afterward I'll go by Dad's office to poke around a little. When I see Kyle, I'll tell him to be sure to call you."

"Oh, no, don't do that," Bess said in alarm. "I don't want him to think I'm clingy. But if *you'd* call me, so I know he's all right . . ."

"I'll try," Nancy promised. "Oops, another call's coming in. I'll catch you later."

The caller was a reporter at one of the local

television stations. He wanted to talk to Carson Drew. Nancy fielded the call as best she could, then left the house for police headquarters.

Detective Washington was out and another detective took her statement. She had to wait to read it over until it was typed, so by the time she reached her dad's office at Judiciary Square it was nearly ten o'clock. After parking in the lot behind the office building, she entered by a back door that led to the lobby. As she made her way to the elevators, she reminded herself to come back to speak to the guard who had been on duty the night before. When the elevator door slid open, she found herself face-to-face with Detective Washington.

"Good morning, Ms. Drew," he said, holding the door open. "I just spoke to my office. Thanks for being prompt with your statement. Oh—when I mentioned your name to one of my colleagues, she said that you've done excellent work as an amateur detective. I just want you to know I don't intend to tolerate any meddling with this case. Is that clear?"

"Of course," Nancy said, and stepped into the elevator. She convinced herself on the ride up that her definition of meddling and his might be a bit different.

Upstairs, she found Carla, the receptionist, with a tissue in one hand and the telephone receiver in the other. Her eyes were red. In a voice that quavered, she was saying, "No public statement at this time. Maybe later in the day."

She hung up and started to greet Nancy as the phone rang again. Nancy gave her a wave and walked to Ms. Hanson's desk. Her father's secretary also appeared to be quite shaken.

"What a terrible way to die," Ms. Hanson said. When Nancy looked blank, she added, "Don't you know how it happened? Detective Washington just told us. The killer hit poor Jack from behind with a law book. His neck broke. Just the thought of it makes me ill—"

It took the woman a few seconds to collect herself, but once she did, she asked, "Are you here to see your father? He just finished with that detective, and now he's over at the courthouse going over the evidence for his case later today."

"That's okay—I'll catch him later," Nancy replied. "Have the police finished their work here?"

Ms. Hanson looked around, as if she hoped to find the answer written on her office wall. "I think so. They searched the offices pretty thoroughly. They even watched while Sylvia inventoried all the securities in the vault. You'll be glad to hear that none was missing. Poor Jack must have surprised the intruder before he managed to open the vault."

"Which office was Broughton using?" Nancy asked.

"Why—just past the reception area, second on the left," Ms. Hanson said.

"I'd like to take a quick look around it."

Ms. Hanson hesitated before saying, "I'm sure that would be all right."

Nancy started for the door, then turned and added, "Oh—and would you mind making me a photocopy of Jack Broughton's résumé?"

This time Ms. Hanson hesitated even longer. "All right, dear," she finally said. "But I'll check with your father first, if you don't mind."

"Of course not," Nancy said quickly. "I'll see you later."

Nancy walked down the corridor to Broughton's office and started for the door. She froze at the sound of a faint noise inside. Taking a deep breath, she pushed the door open wide.

The room was just big enough for a desk, a chair, and a table. No place for an intruder to hide, except—Nancy stepped back to look through the crack between the open door and the frame and suppressed a gasp. Someone was lurking behind the door!

Chapter

Four

Nancy GAVE THE DOOR a hard shove, and the person hiding behind it grunted. Taking advantage of the moment, she entered the room and said, "Come out of there, before I call the police."

"No, wait," a familiar voice pleaded. Kyle Donovan stepped out from behind the door. His eyes were wide with what Nancy thought must be fear.

"Oh, hello, Nancy," he said with an awkward laugh when he recognized her. "I didn't expect to find you here."

"I bet you didn't," Nancy muttered under her breath. Aloud, she said, "Is there something you need from this office? Maybe I can find it for you."

"Er—just a file," Kyle replied. "I thought it might be here, but it's not. It doesn't matter. See you."

"Wait, Kyle," she said, closing the door behind her. "Take a seat," she added.

Kyle sat in the only chair as Nancy perched on the corner of the desk.

"I'm glad I ran into you," she said. "I need to ask you some questions. First of all, what kind of guy was Jack Broughton?"

"Broughton?" Kyle repeated, casting his gaze away from Nancy. "I don't know. I hardly knew him. He hadn't been here long, you know. You're the one who found him last night, aren't you?"

Nancy nodded.

Kyle shifted on his chair. "It was just luck that I wasn't here myself," he said, now staring at one of the corners.

"Oh?" Nancy said encouragingly.

"Fact. I thought I was going to have to work late, but then I finished sooner than I expected. So I decided to take in a flick—*Danger by Moonlight*. It's playing over at the Keith. I had no idea it was such a long movie. By the time it was over, the only thing I felt like doing was going home to bed."

"And that's what you did," Nancy concluded.

"Exactly," Kyle replied. "Well, back to the grindstone. If you see Bess, tell her I'll give her a call, okay?"

"I'll do that," Nancy said coolly as he backed out. She shut the door after him, then stood in the center of the small room, her mind full of questions.

What was it in the room that Kyle had come to find? His story of looking for a file might be true, but if so, there didn't seem to be anything casual about his need for it.

Second point: If he had finished work early the night before, why hadn't he called Bess? Were things not going well between the two of them, or did he have some other problem?

Most interesting, though, was why he had gone to such lengths to make sure that Nancy knew where he had been the night before. When somebody took the trouble to produce an alibi before he'd even been accused of anything, Nancy had to ask if he might have a guilty conscience.

Could Kyle be Broughton's killer? Except for the suspiciously well-timed alibi, there was nothing to say that he *wasn't*. What would drive him to such a desperate move? The answer, if there was one, might be somewhere in this room. Nancy threw back her shoulders, took a deep breath, and began to search the desk.

It didn't take long—the desk had only one drawer. Aside from a handful of pens and pencils and a tangle of paper clips, it seemed to hold only a bunch of paper napkins and sugar packets from the coffee shop downstairs. Nancy was about to close the drawer when she noticed a small scratch pad. It was blank, but when she looked at it from an angle, she could see indentations from what had been written on the top page, which was now torn off. It was a list of some sort. The first item was "R21304." Each of the other items also consisted of a letter and five numbers. She carefully copied them into her notebook, made sure she left the office the way she had found it, and went out to Ms. Hanson's desk.

"Is there any way of knowing who has been using which files?" she asked.

"Why, of course there is," Ms. Hanson answered. "Margaret Hildebrand, the librarian, keeps a complete log showing which files are out and who has them. It's very important, you know."

"I imagine so," Nancy said. "And if I want a certain file, I should go to her?"

Ms. Hanson nodded. "That's right. Ordinarily, she's right in the library, but the police moved her to an empty office down the hall. Number four. Oh, I went ahead and made that photocopy for you. Here it is."

She held out an envelope.

Nancy smiled. "Thanks," she said, tucking it in her purse.

Margaret Hildebrand was in her mid-twenties, with short black hair and startlingly blue eyes.

She listened to Nancy's request, then produced a large canvas-bound ledger.

"Lots of luck," she said. "Jack checked out dozens of files every day. They're all accounted for, of course, but there are a lot of transactions for you to check."

The first thing Nancy noticed was that each file was identified by a letter, followed by five numbers. "Do any of these look familiar?" she asked, handing Margaret the list she had copied from the scratch pad.

Margaret scanned the list. "I really couldn't say," she replied. "Once I locate a file and log it out, I forget it. If I didn't, my mind would be cluttered before the end of the week. Are these the files you need to consult?"

"If it's not too much trouble," Nancy said.

"That's what I'm here for," Margaret said. "But I am a little backlogged at the moment. How's this afternoon?"

"Fine, and thanks," Nancy said. As she walked away, she considered her next move. Broughton's office had yielded one possible clue. Why not try his home? She opened the envelope Ms. Hanson had given her and checked the address on Broughton's résumé before going down in the elevator.

She was crossing the lobby when someone called, "Nancy! Nancy Drew!"

Nancy stopped and rolled her eyes before turning around. She knew that voice. It belonged to Brenda Carlton. Brenda liked to think of herself as an ace reporter. Everyone else thought of her as a grade-A pest. She wrote for a newspaper that happened to belong to her father.

"Nancy," Brenda said, grabbing her arm. "I've been trying to reach you all morning. I need a statement from you on how it felt to find a dead body in your father's plush downtown office."

Nancy disengaged her arm and said in a level voice, "Sorry, no comment."

"Is it true that millions of dollars in securities are missing from the firm's vault?" Brenda continued.

Nancy held her tongue and started to walk away.

Brenda kept up with her. "What about the theory that the burglary and murder were part of a scheme to cover up the fact that the securities are missing? Any reaction to that?"

Nancy turned and took a deep breath. She was on the point of telling Brenda exactly what she thought of her stupid theories and slimy innuendos when the smirk on Brenda's face reminded Nancy that this was exactly the reaction Brenda was trying to provoke with her outrageous exaggerations.

"Sorry, no comment," Nancy said once more, and headed for the door and her car. Brenda followed her the whole way, only backing off when it looked as if Nancy were about to close the car door on her hand.

Broughton's apartment was about ten minutes away in a garden complex that was run-down and seedy. His front door had a police seal pasted across the lock, but there were no squad cars outside, leading Nancy to hope that the police had already come and gone. She backed away and carefully studied the building, then she went around to the rear and started counting back doors. When she came to the one that should lead to Broughton's apartment, she tapped on the glass, waited, and tapped again. No response. She glanced both ways, then took a lock pick from her purse and inserted it in the keyhole.

After a tense moment, she heard a welcome click, and the door swung open. She slipped inside and closed it quietly behind her. The silence had a heavy quality, as if the apartment had been empty for months. Only the dish and cup on the drainboard and the newspaper on the kitchen table testified that someone had lived here—and not too long ago.

Moving steadily, Nancy started to explore. In the living room she noticed an expensive stereo, but no CDs or cassettes. The TV was enormous, with an elaborate VCR perched on a shelf next to it, but no tapes. The only book in sight was a best-selling photo essay about the fantasies and nightmares of a celebrated rock star.

Shaking her head, she decided to try the bedroom. The bed was unmade, and the cops who'd searched the dresser and the old-fashioned rolltop desk in the corner had not done a very good job of putting things back. A stack of typing paper was sitting on the desk chair, and a few sheets had spilled onto the light blue carpet.

Nancy picked up the pages and glanced at them. They were all blank. She set them on the desk, then opened the door to the closet and let out a low whistle. At least ten suits and as many sport jackets hung there, along with dozens of shirts and sweaters. Lined up on the floor were several pairs of highly polished shoes.

She moved closer and reached for one of the jackets with an expensive designer label. As she did, she felt a violent shove in the small of her back. She stumbled forward, straight into the clothes. Behind her, the closet door was slammed shut. She twisted around quickly to push at it with all her force, but it refused to move.

The interior of the closet was totally dark, and the shoe polish air was stuffy. The corner of a hanger poked Nancy in the back of the neck. She felt as if the unseen walls were closing in on her.

Nancy Drew, get a grip on yourself, she thought. She took a deep breath, then began to consider her situation, step by step. Someone had pushed her into the closet and locked her in.

What was keeping the door locked? Closet doors didn't usually have locks. She ran her hand up and down the edge of the door and found a small knob. It turned easily. At half a turn, she could feel the tongue of the latch clearing the lock plate, but the door remained stubbornly closed. She was beginning to think that someone had wedged a chair under the doorknob outside, in which case Nancy had no idea how she'd get out. The minutes seemed to drag.

Suddenly, out of sheer frustration, Nancy reached behind her and pushed the suits and shirts all the way down to one side and out of her way. Grasping the small knob in her left hand, she disengaged the latch, then leaned against the door and shoved. Was she imagining that it moved just a fraction of an inch? She released the pressure, then shoved again. It didn't budge at all.

She sank back against the wall, wondering if she'd eventually pass out in her almost airless prison and how many minutes had gone by—five, ten? She couldn't judge. It felt like ages.

It seemed hopeless, but she decided to pound on the door with her fist.

When she stopped she heard a sound. Was it a door opening somewhere in the apartment? And were those footsteps coming toward the closet?

Chapter

Five

WITH NO WARNING, the door swung open. Caught off-guard, Nancy half fell out of the closet. She squinted to protect her eyes from the sudden glare of daylight.

"Nancy Drew!" a voice exclaimed. "What on earth—"

Nancy recognized David Megali, the young journalist she had met the night before. He was holding a chair—the one that had imprisoned her, Nancy realized. Relief flowed through her like a tide.

"David," she cried. "What are you doing here?"

"Rescuing you from a closet, for a start," he replied with a lopsided smile. "No, seriously, I bet I'm here for almost the same reason you are. I still think that Broughton was the anonymous caller who offered me an important lead for my nursing-home story. And I bet you're trying to track down his killer, right?"

Nancy nodded. "But how did you get the address?" she asked.

David arched his eyebrows. "I called the police department and read them the lead of my story about Broughton's death, complete with an address I made up. So, of course, they corrected me."

Nancy couldn't help but laugh.

"And when I got here," he went on, "I found the back door unlocked and you trapped in this closet."

"Someone must have been in the apartment when I came in," Nancy hypothesized. "And whoever it was was so worried about being found here that he or she shoved me into the closet. I'm going to take a look around for any trace of my mystery assailant." She found the bathroom door slightly ajar. Hadn't it been shut earlier? she wondered. She moved over to it. The bathroom was empty, but she spotted a scuff mark, like a footprint, on the white enamel floor of the shower. Her attacker must have hidden there when he heard her entering the apartment, then rushed out when her back was turned. She knelt down to study the mark, but it was too smudged to be of any use.

As she got back to her feet, she caught a whiff of a lemony scent that was somehow familiar. Where had she smelled it before? In Broughton's office, perhaps? She checked the cabinet over the sink and found three different brands of aftershave, but none of them was lemon scented. She returned to the shower stall and noticed the scent again.

A scene flashed into her mind of Bess telling her that she planned to buy Kyle a special brand of cologne for his birthday. Then she had added, with a laugh, that she hoped he didn't use too much, though—that sometimes she could walk into a room and know he'd been there by the lingering scent.

Did Nancy remember Kyle's scent from her interview with him that morning? It was possible, but the harder she tried to decide, the less sure she was. She gave up and went back to the bedroom.

"What is it?" David asked. He was standing at the desk, shuffling through the papers there. "Did you find anything?"

"Nothing worth talking about," Nancy reported. "How about you?"

"Nothing," he replied.

Nancy returned to the closet and began searching the jackets hanging there. She patted all of them, without any results, but as she returned them to their places, she heard a sound like the rustling of paper. She pulled a soft tweed jacket out and examined it. It was mostly gray with flecks of light blue. She plunged her hand into each of the patch pockets, then into the breast pocket. All she found was a dime. She left it there and opened the jacket. It had inside pockets on both sides, but they, too, were empty. She was about to hang it back in the closet when she noticed, lower down on the left side of the inner lining, another, smaller pocket, about the right size for a cigarette lighter.

Holding her breath, Nancy dipped her fingers into it. A grin spread over her face as she pulled out a slip of paper. She put the jacket away and unfolded the paper. In bold, spiky letters, someone—presumably Broughton—had printed

DAM ALF SG
KY D 100/WK?

"What did you find?" David asked.

"I don't know," Nancy replied, puzzling over the note. Then something jumped out at her: "KY D"—*Kyle Donovan!* But what did "100/WK?" mean? A hundred a week? Had Broughton been planning to pay Kyle a hundred dollars a week for some reason, or hoping to get Kyle to pay *him* that amount? Either way, it added up to a lot of money.

Nancy looked at the closet full of new de-

43

signer clothes and recalled all the expensive electronic equipment in the living room. How *had* Broughton afforded all that stuff? She imagined he made a decent salary, but not that much. And above all, why would someone murder him?

One theory answered all her questions. If Jack Broughton had been a blackmailer, and if Kyle had been one of his victims . . . !

"I have to go," Nancy said to David. "Are you coming?"

"Hey, slow down," he said, putting his hands on her upper arms. "I thought we were going to be a team."

Nancy glanced up at his brown eyes with the little flecks of gold. He seemed to be almost disappointed in her.

"We are," she began.

"So what did you just figure out? I could tell it was something."

Nancy definitely didn't want to mention her suspicions about Kyle at this point, but she also didn't want to discourage David from helping. Given his experience, he might prove useful. In fact, he already had. He'd let her out of the closet.

She shifted her weight, smiled at him, and said, "Look, I just have to run something down. As soon as I do, I'll let you know what I find out."

He nodded and took a step back. Then he grinned. "How about over dinner tonight?"

"Well—" An image of Ned flashed in her

mind, but then she decided Ned would understand. "Sure. When and where?"

"The Riverside Restaurant? I hear it's good," he said. "Around eight?"

"You're on," Nancy said. "Now let's see about getting out of here without attracting any attention."

Back at her father's office, Nancy said hi to Carla and asked, "Is Kyle Donovan in?"

"Why, yes, he just got back half an hour ago," Carla replied.

"Oh? He was out of the office for a while?" Nancy asked, in as casual a voice as she could manage.

Carla nodded. "Sure. He was looking up some documents over at the Hall of Records," she said. "He's really tops at doing searches."

I bet, Nancy muttered to herself. But at the Hall of Records? Or at Jack Broughton's apartment? When she realized that Bess might be involved with a murder suspect, she felt sick to her stomach.

Aloud, she said, "Do you think he's busy now? I'd like to talk to him for a few minutes."

"Do you want me to buzz him?" Carla asked.

"No, that's okay. I'll just poke my head in."

She found Kyle in the library, at the long oak table stacked high with law books. He was busy making notes on a legal pad. At least a dozen pages already covered with notes were in an untidy pile on his right.

"Kyle?" Nancy said. "Sorry to interrupt, but I need to talk to you."

He straightened up, put down his pen, and ran his fingers through his curly blond hair. "I'm pretty busy, Nancy," he said. "This is something I have to get done today. Can it wait?"

"No, but it doesn't have to take long, if you're frank with me." She closed the door behind her and took a deep breath, fully aware that she was betting a lot on a hunch. "Why were you making regular payments to Jack Broughton?" she asked.

Kyle's eyes widened and his jaw dropped. An instant later he recovered and said, "That's crazy. Why would I do that?"

"That was *my* question," Nancy pointed out. Taking a chance and stretching the truth a bit, she added, "I have evidence that you were paying Broughton one hundred dollars a week. That's a lot of money for you. What were you buying with it? His silence?"

Kyle stared at her as if hypnotized.

"What did he have on you?" Nancy probed. "Something in your past that would ruin your chances of getting into law school if it came out? That's it, isn't it? I can see that's it. It's written all over your face."

"All I have to say is this," Kyle said, narrowing

his eyes. "Whoever rid the world of Jack Broughton deserves a medal!"

With that he went back to his law books.

"What did he have on you, Kyle?" Nancy repeated softly. "I won't tell anyone, I promise. You have my word."

He remained turned away from her, but she could see the tension in his back.

"I'm asking you first, Kyle," she continued, "because I care about you. Bess is a very special friend of mine, and I don't want to see her hurt. But if I have to, I'll start asking other people. I'd rather not, because just asking questions can start rumors. So I'd like to hear it straight from you. What was Broughton holding over you?"

Kyle searched her face, as if asking himself if he dared trust her. At last he gave a sharp nod. "A lot," he said almost in a whisper. "A whole lot."

"Something serious, you mean?"

He gave an odd laugh. "Is homicide serious enough for you? I was tried as a juvenile, and the records were supposedly sealed, but Broughton managed to ferret it all out."

"You killed somebody?" Nancy asked in horror.

"No, as a matter of fact, I didn't. But I couldn't prove it," he replied. "If only . . ."

He covered his face with his hands for a moment, then took them down and said, "What happened was this. I was leaving a basketball game one night with my friend Terry. We were both fourteen. And this guy we knew—Jim, an eleventh-grader—offered us a ride in this fancy car. We figured it was his father's, right? How were we supposed to know he'd stolen it?"

He stopped to rub the back of his neck, then continued. "So we're cruising along, listening to a tape, when a cop gets on our tail and turns on the blinkers. Jim steps on it and tries to lose the cop, but he skids on some wet leaves and wraps the car around a big tree. Terry's thrown out and killed instantly, and I've got a broken arm and glass cuts all over my face. Wouldn't you know it? Jim wasn't touched. And while I'm lying there in pain, he crawls past me and shoves me over behind the wheel, to make it look like *I* was the driver!"

"Oh, no, how awful!" Nancy exclaimed. "The police didn't believe him, did they?"

Kyle's face and voice were eerily calm as he said, "I think they must have suspected the truth, but they couldn't prove it any more than I could. It was a matter of my word against Jim's. In the end, his lawyer got him off with a plea of grand theft—auto, and I was put on two years' probation. Of course, I stayed out of trouble for those two years, and eventually the whole thing was mostly forgotten. Until Broughton came along, that is."

Nancy said, "I can see why you're bitter. But why were you willing to buy his silence? You didn't do anything to be ashamed of."

"Look at it this way," he replied. "You're on a committee that's looking over law school applications. You've got ten applicants for every spot. It figures you'll cross people off any way you can, right? And if you're choosing between two people who've got about the same qualifications, and someone named Jack Broughton gives you evidence that one of them might just be an ex–car thief who was responsible for the death of his best friend, then your decision about who to pick gets a lot easier."

"That's not fair!" Nancy burst out. "But I do hear what you're saying."

"And what would the cops think if they found and started checking out my record?" Kyle continued. "I can't believe they believe that burglary story any more than I do. So here I am, a ready-made fall guy with a record. Even if they didn't find enough evidence to indict me, the word would get around, and I'd always be under suspicion. I can kiss my legal career goodbye, at the least."

Nancy filed his comments away for further study and said, "But, Kyle, once the police learn that Broughton was a blackmailer, it will open up lots of suspects and possibilities. Maybe he learned something from the files here and was using it against somebody. This somebody may have killed him instead of paying the blackmail. I can't believe you're the first person he black-mailed. I bet he was blackmailing people at his last job, too, and one of them might have fol-lowed him to River Heights."

Kyle's face brightened for a moment, then fell again. "Nice try, Nancy," he said. "But there's still the matter of my record. Once that comes out, I'm finished, even if I do have an alibi for the time of Broughton's murder."

"You told me you were at the movies," Nancy said. "Er—what was it you said you saw?"

Something in her tone must have alerted him. He looked up at her with sharpened attention and said, *"Danger by Moonlight*. It's playing at the Keith. What's the matter—you want me to tell you the plot?"

Nancy shook her head. "I'm sorry, Kyle. *Dan-ger by Moonlight was* playing at the Keith, but it closed two days ago. Now they're showing some-thing called *Avenue of Shame."*

"Oh, right." He gave a nervous laugh. "I must have gotten the titles mixed up."

Nancy studied her hands. "And the plots, too?" she asked. "I don't think so. I'm sorry, Kyle, but I don't believe you were at the movies last night. And that makes me wonder what you *were* doing at the time Jack Broughton was killed."

He pushed his chair back and stood up. Nancy took a step back, toward the door.

"That's what you're wondering, is it?" Kyle said in a tone that oozed menace. "I don't think you're wondering at all. Your mind's made up already. You've already tried and convicted me, haven't you? Well, fine."

He took a step in her direction, and Nancy got ready to defend herself against a sudden attack.

"But let me tell you something," he continued. "If you're really interested in finding the person who killed Jack Broughton, you won't have to go far from home. Because the murderer is none other than the eminent attorney Mr. Carson Drew, your father."

Chapter

Six

NANCY WAS FURIOUS. How dare Kyle accuse her father of being a murderer! Her father was one of the most respected citizens of River Heights. She almost slipped and started to yell at him but stopped herself just in time. She was in the middle of an investigation and couldn't afford to let her emotions interfere with her judgment in the case.

"That's an extremely serious charge," she said icily. "You'd better be able to back it up."

"You bet I can," he replied angrily. "And don't think I'm happy about this. Carson Drew was a hero of mine—until last night. Now I don't know what to think."

"What makes you think my father is connected to Broughton's death?" she demanded.

Kyle turned his back on her and walked toward one of the bookshelves. As he fingered the spine of a volume of appellate court decisions, he said, "This may take a minute, but let me do it in my own way. You're right about one thing. I *didn't* go to that movie last night. I saw it a few nights ago." He turned toward Nancy, almost pleading with her. "It was the first thing that came to mind when I thought I needed an alibi. The truth is, I spent most of the time in question downstairs, across the street from the entrance to the building."

"Why? What were you doing there?"

"Trying to work up the nerve to come up here and tell Broughton to go jump in the lake," he said bitterly. "I knew it meant the end of my dream of becoming a lawyer, but I couldn't stand to let that leech go on sucking my blood!"

"And when did you finally come back up here?" Nancy asked.

"I didn't," he replied. He held out his hands in a gesture that begged for her understanding. "I couldn't do it! I kept telling myself that I could find a better way out of the trap I was in, that I didn't have to give up everything. But deep down I knew that I just didn't have the guts to confront him and let everything come out."

"Exactly when were you across the street?"

"I left the office between five and five-thirty," he said. "I meant to come back after everybody left. I grabbed a sandwich in the coffee shop, then stood in a doorway down the block, arguing with myself, for a long time. Finally I just went home."

"'A long time'?" Nancy quoted. "How long? An hour? Two hours?"

Kyle glanced to either side, as if expecting to find an answer there. "I don't know," he said. "When did you get here? I left right after I saw you show up. I was afraid you'd see me and mention it to Bess. I had told her I had to work late, you know."

Nancy nodded. "All right. I got here at seven, give or take a minute or two. And you were watching the entrance the whole time, from just after five-thirty until seven? That makes you a very important witness, Kyle. You probably saw the murderer!"

"I think I did," he said wearily. "I already told you. Your father showed up a little before six. I was surprised to see him because I knew he was supposed to be out of town. He arrived in a taxi, with a briefcase and a small suitcase, and went into the building. And when I went home, he still hadn't come out!"

Nancy stared at him. "That's impossible!" she declared. "He wasn't in the office when I went upstairs. You must have been seeing things!"

"Maybe he hid when he heard you coming," Kyle said. "Because I do know I saw him go into the building. I thought it was odd for him to show up then, but I didn't really think about it until this morning when I found out about Broughton."

"This morning? Or last night?" Nancy said. "I have only your word that you were down in the street all that time." Nancy, who rarely got angry, found herself on the verge of losing her temper. "Did you go up to the office after all and have your face-off with Broughton? Maybe he pushed you a little too far. Is that the way it was, Kyle? And maybe this story about my father is made up to keep people from noticing that you had both the opportunity and the motive to kill Jack Broughton."

Kyle's face reddened and he took a quick step toward her, fists raised to the level of his chest. "You're not going to frame me for this murder, Nancy Drew," he lashed out. "Don't think you will. I'll fight you any way I can."

Nancy jumped aside as he stormed out the door. For a moment she considered going after him, but what was the point? She couldn't force him to talk.

She knew it had been a mistake to accuse him like that. Ordinarily, she might have kept her suspicions to herself to avoid spooking him, but she wasn't at her best just then. She had to admit that Kyle's story about her father had rattled her.

Why on earth had he invented such a lie?

Carson Drew had given Kyle his first real job, with real responsibilities, in a real law firm. Kyle ought to be grateful to him. Instead he was throwing mud at him.

Nancy asked herself how well she really knew Kyle. Not very well, it seemed. He certainly wasn't acting like the same guy she had arranged to date one of her best friends! Unless . . .

What if he sincerely believed he had seen her father entering the building? It had been dark, after all. He could easily have made a mistake, especially if he only caught a glimpse from the side or the back.

The explanation made sense, but how could she persuade Kyle that it was right? The way he felt about her right then, he probably wouldn't listen to her even if she were screaming "Fire!"

One person might convince him—her father. If he told Kyle where he had been the evening before, Kyle would have to admit his mistake. It had to be done at once, Nancy knew. Kyle had to be stopped before he spread the damaging story.

Nancy picked up the phone on the library table and dialed an extension. "Ms. Hanson, it's Nancy. Is my father still at the courthouse? You don't happen to know the room number, do you? Okay, thanks."

The courthouse was just three minutes away, on the opposite side of Judiciary Square. Nancy walked briskly, breathing in the crisp, pure air and admiring the classical silhouette of the court-house against a brilliant sky. Leaves of red, yellow, and russet skittered across the sidewalk, urged on by the light breeze.

She spotted her father just outside a court-room, talking with another attorney. He spotted her, too, and beckoned her over.

"Frank, you've met my daughter, Nancy, haven't you?" he asked, putting an arm around her shoulder.

"I certainly have," Frank replied, smiling. "I'm a big fan of her work, too. Working on a new case, Nancy?"

Before she could answer, Frank's smile had vanished. "Oh, I'm terribly sorry, Carson. Forgive me. I heard the news this morning about that young man in your firm, but it slipped my mind. Excuse me, I'd better run."

Carson watched him go, then turned back to Nancy. "It's been that way all morning," he said in a tired voice. "People don't know the right thing to say, so they avoid me altogether or get away from me as soon as possible.

"Never mind," he added stoically. "They'll get over it. Would you like to have a little late lunch with me?"

"That sounds great," Nancy replied, glad for a reason to postpone questioning him.

As they walked back across the square to the coffee shop, Carson said, "This liability case is starting to look tough. Never mind. No talking business at lunch—it ruins the digestion."

After a brief wait they got a booth, and Carson ordered a large salad and an iced tea. Nancy asked for a grilled cheese and tomato sandwich, french fries, and a root beer.

Her father made a face. "You're so lucky. You don't have to worry about your weight or your cholesterol," he remarked. "Or your digestion."

"Yet!" Nancy replied, laughing. Then, taking a deep breath, she said, "Dad? There's something I need to talk to you about. Kyle told me that he saw you arrive at the office yesterday evening at a little before six."

Carson looked at her with narrowed eyes. "Nancy, I'm disappointed in you," he said. "I thought you agreed to tell me when you were starting to dig into Jack Broughton's death."

Nancy felt her cheeks grow red at his reproach. "Dad," she said softly but firmly, "you told me you wanted me to tell you what I was doing. Fine. But you can't expect me to check in with you every hour. I have to follow up any leads I come across, the way I would in any case. Sure, this case is different. I'm the one who discovered the body, for one thing. And I'm your daughter. Anything that affects you affects me, too—such as rumors that place you at the scene of the crime."

Her father gave her an odd look. "You mean

place me at my office? Why on earth *shouldn't* I be there?"

Nancy gaped at him. "Well—were you there last night?"

He sat back as the iced tea and soda arrived, then said, "Yes, I was. Just as Kyle told you."

It took Nancy a moment to believe her own ears. "Dad!" she exclaimed. "You were in the office from six o'clock on last night? But—why didn't you tell me? Or the police?"

"Whoa," Carson said, holding up his hand. "Not so fast. First of all, I wasn't there from six *on*, I was there *at* six, or thereabouts. I went by to drop off some things to be typed and to pick up a couple of files I needed to study before going to court today. I don't suppose I was upstairs for more than five or ten minutes, at the most."

Nancy took a moment to let this new information sink in. Then she asked, "What about Jack Broughton? Did you see him?"

"No. I did notice a light in the library, but I didn't go down that way to see who was there. I was too tired, to tell the truth. So I simply picked up what I needed from my office, left the dictation cassettes for Ms. Hanson, and left. Then, on the way home, I stopped at the Heights Café and ate so Hannah wouldn't have the bother of fixing my dinner. I was home by seven-thirty or so."

Their sandwiches arrived. Carson asked for the check, to avoid a delay later.

"But, Dad," Nancy began, "why didn't you say anything about this last night?"

Carson pinched the bridge of his nose, then rubbed his eyes. "Nancy, honey," he said at last. "I was very, very tired last night. And when you told me about Jack, I was shocked. It just didn't occur to me."

Nancy took a bite of her sandwich and frowned. "One thing I don't understand," she said. "Kyle says he didn't see you leave."

"He was keeping the building under surveillance? How peculiar," Carson said, surprised. "Well, he obviously doesn't know there's a door out the back of the lobby to the parking lot. I went out that way because I'd left my car in the lot while I was out of town.

"We'd better eat and get back," he added. "My case has been recessed until tomorrow, but I've got a load of work to tackle."

As they left the coffee shop, Nancy said, "You'd better tell the police you were at the office last night, Dad, and right away. You might have been on the spot when Jack Broughton was killed."

"I realize that," he replied. "Actually, I did tell that detective this morning. He seemed very concerned about my admission. I hope I'm wrong, but I'm afraid I might be a suspect in this murder case."

* * *

The reception area of Carson Drew's office seemed jammed with large men. When Nancy counted, she realized there were only five of them. One of the five was Detective Washington.

"Oh, Mr. Drew," Ms. Hanson said, her face filled with relief. "I wasn't sure when you'd be back. These gentlemen—"

Washington stepped forward. "Mr. Drew?" he said. "Could you spare me a little more time, sir? Some questions have been raised about your possible involvement in the death of Jack Broughton."

"Involvement, Detective?" Carson repeated. "I can't say I like your choice of words."

"Yes, sir," Washington said. "Er—the suggestion has been made that there may be some irregularities in your financial dealings with your elderly clients and that the deceased discovered this and threatened to bring it to public notice. Do you have any comment?"

"I certainly do," Carson said vigorously. "It is pure slander and totally without foundation. And I'd like very much to know the source of this so-called suggestion. I'm sure it's no one reputable."

"I'm afraid I can't really say anything about that," the detective said, looking uncomfortable. "Would you have any objection if we took a closer look around your offices?"

"Of course not," Carson replied.

"I'd also like to send part of my team to check around your home," Washington added. "It's just a matter of covering all bases. You understand."

"I think I'm beginning to," Carson said. Nancy could hear the anger and disbelief in her father's voice, though she was sure anyone else would have thought he was totally calm. "And I must tell you I deeply resent the implication. But please go ahead. Search as thoroughly as you like. I have nothing whatever to hide!"

Chapter

Seven

As WASHINGTON'S officers fanned out through the suite, Nancy sat with her father in his office. He picked up a file and opened it. After one impatient glance, he slapped it down on the desk.

"Honestly," he said with barely suppressed anger. "This is utter nonsense! Washington may be a good detective, but he doesn't know his way around River Heights yet if he believes a ridiculous rumor like this."

Nancy cleared her throat and said, "Dad? Is it possible that there's something to the story?"

He stared at her in disbelief. "What! You think I killed Jack Broughton because he found out that I'm fleecing my elderly clients?"

"No, of course not," Nancy protested. "But

suppose there *is* some sort of scam going on at the expense of old people and some of them are your clients. Broughton might have found out about it and tried to blackmail whoever's behind it. That might be enough of a motive for his murder."

"Agreed," Carson said. "But do you have any reason to believe that—aside from this ridiculous tip that Washington received?"

"Maybe," Nancy said slowly. She told him about David Megali and the anonymous phone call that had brought him to the law firm the evening before.

"Megali?" Carson repeated. "I don't recognize the name, but if he's not from around here, there's no reason I should. What magazine did you say he writes for?"

When Nancy told him the name, he picked up the telephone and asked Ms. Hanson to put him through to the magazine's editorial offices in New York. A minute later he said to Nancy, "I imagine your Mr. Megali is exactly who he says he is, but there's no harm—"

He broke off as the phone buzzed. He identified himself to the person on the other end and explained why he was calling. After a brief conversation, he hung up and said, "They've published a couple of articles by Megali. The editor I spoke to said the magazine is very interested in his nursing-home story."

"That's good to know," Nancy said. "I'd hate to think that I'd been taken in by a con artist. By the way, Dad, I know you have a lot to do this afternoon. If Detective Washington still wants to check out our house, why don't you let me take him over? It'd be one less thing for you to worry about."

And it'll give me a chance to keep tabs on what the police are doing, she added to herself.

"You don't mind?" her father said, the relief sounding in his voice. "It would be a help."

"No problem," Nancy replied, and settled down to wait.

Twenty minutes later the team of detectives finished their search, and Detective Washington came to Carson's office. His disgruntled expression made it clear that he had not found anything important.

"Thank you for your cooperation, Mr. Drew," the detective said. His tone didn't sound grateful, though.

"Citizens should cooperate with the police," Carson replied. "And as an officer of the court, I have an even greater responsibility to do so. Do you still intend to search my home, Detective?"

Washington shifted nervously from one foot to the other. "With your permission, Mr. Drew," he replied.

"Of course," Carson said. "My daughter will go with you and show you around."

For a moment the detective looked as if he were about to argue, but then he must have realized that without a search warrant he was on very shaky ground. "Thanks," he said, glancing over at Nancy. "We can go now, if that's okay with you."

Washington and two of his men followed Nancy's Mustang in an unmarked car. Once home, she pulled into the driveway and Washington pulled up at the curb behind a car already parked there. As they got out, so did the passengers of the other car. With a sinking heart, Nancy saw that it was Brenda Carlton and a guy with a camera.

Nancy hurried over in time to hear Brenda ask, "Detective Washington, is it true that the prominent attorney Carson Drew has been systematically looting the trust accounts of helpless elderly clients?"

"No comment," Washington said as the photographer took a shot of him and Brenda with the house in the background. "Excuse me. I have work to do."

He started to move away, and Brenda followed, as did the photographer. "Are you here to search the Drew house?" Brenda demanded. "You're in charge of the investigation of the brutal murder of Jack Broughton. Is it true that Carson Drew is your prime suspect?"

"No comment," Washington repeated, and

strode up to walk toward the house. Nancy started to follow him, but Brenda stepped in front of her.

"As the daughter of a murder suspect—" she began.

Nancy cut her off. "I am the daughter of Carson Drew, but my father is *not* a murder suspect. Now please get out of my way and off our lawn." She brushed past the reporter and quickly walked toward her house.

Brenda shouted after her. "Are you going to try to find someone else to take the blame for this crime?"

Stung, Nancy whirled around. "I am going to do my best to find out the truth about it," she proclaimed. "If that means fixing the blame on the real criminal, great!"

As she spoke, the photographer crouched down and fired off three or four frames of her glaring at Brenda.

Terrific, Nancy thought, as she turned away again. If one of those pictures is printed in Brenda's paper, I'll probably be offered the role of the Wicked Witch of the West in a remake of *The Wizard of Oz!*

Nancy caught up with the team of searchers in the front hall. Hannah, confused by the sudden invasion of the house, was asking them if they would like tea or coffee. Nancy was glad to see this offer of hospitality embarrassed Washington.

"No, thanks, ma'am," he said. "If we could just look around?"

"My father's study is this way," Nancy offered. "That's probably where you want to start."

She showed them in, then returned to the living room. She needed time to think over some puzzling questions. Who had tipped off Brenda that the police were going to search the Drew house? Not to mention feeding her all that nonsense about Nancy's father robbing his elderly clients?

Why had Washington decided to conduct the searches? Not because of any hard evidence— that was pretty obvious. If he really had such evidence, he wouldn't have had to ask Carson's permission to search the office and house. Instead he would have taken the evidence to a judge and gotten a search warrant. That suggested that the police detective was acting solely on the basis of a tip, and *that* suggested that the same person had tipped off the police and Brenda. Having two tipsters in the same case, with the same idea at the same time, was stretching coincidence a bit too far.

Who was this mysterious tipster? The person had to be familiar with the inner workings of Carson Drew's law firm and the police investigation of Broughton's murder. Nancy was afraid she knew who the obvious candidate was—Kyle Donovan. He had accused Carson of murder to

Nancy's face. Why should he hesitate to do the same to the press or the police?

His motive, Nancy decided, was obvious, too. If he could manage to divert the attention of the police to Carson Drew, they might fail to notice that he had a powerful motive and the opportunity to kill Broughton. Still, Nancy wasn't ready to believe Kyle was a murderer.

What should be the next step in her investigation then? She knew that Broughton had been blackmailing Kyle and why. Was Kyle his only victim though? It didn't seem likely. Nancy decided the place to look for clues to the identity of other victims was in the files that Broughton had been consulting.

Nancy picked up the telephone and called the office. "Carla? It's Nancy. Could I speak to Margaret Hildebrand? Thanks."

When the firm librarian came on the line, Nancy asked if the files she had requested were available. They were.

"All of them? Great! Thanks," Nancy said. "I'll be in later this afternoon."

Nancy hung up and turned to find Detective Washington standing in the doorway about six feet away. He had obviously overheard her conversation. Her accusing stare made him lower his eyes.

"We're all done here, Nancy," he said. "Thanks for your cooperation."

"You didn't find anything, did you?" Nancy observed. "Of course, you can't answer, but we both know you couldn't have found anything because there wasn't anything for you to find. Somebody's been playing practical jokes on you. And personally, I don't think they're funny," she added, glancing out the window. A TV remote unit had just pulled up in front of the house.

"No, I agree," Washington replied, following the direction of her gaze. "Believe me, it's not fun for us, either. But we have a job to do, and believe it or not, we generally do it pretty well."

Nancy opened the front door for him and his team. She was careful to stay out of range of the TV camera. She knew that unless the TV crew got good pictures the story would be useless to them.

Once Washington and his officers were gone, Nancy lay down on the couch and closed her eyes. She found it impossible to relax and after a few minutes got up to call Ned. Nancy could always rely on Ned to help her clarify her thinking. There was no answer so Nancy hung up and headed back downtown to her dad's law office.

The files were laid out for her on the long oak table in the library. She slowly leafed through each of them, searching for anything that might link up with the case. Two of them concerned elderly clients, but neither involved large sums of money. The other files were a divorce, an adoption, a personal-injury case, and a couple of commercial real-estate transactions. She didn't spot any obvious possibilities for blackmail among them.

Frustrated, she left the office and went back downstairs. As she was crossing the lobby, she spotted the night security guard on his way in. She waved and went up to him.

"Terrible thing, what happened last night," he said. "You found him, I hear. Terrible thing."

"Yes, it was," Nancy replied. "I wanted to ask you about any other people who went up to my dad's office last night."

"The cops already asked me," he said, nodding. "I told them what I'll tell you. There weren't any—not after seven, when I started logging people in. Before that, I wouldn't know."

"No one at all?" Nancy asked, not bothering to mask her disappointment.

"Nope. Not unless you count the cops themselves and that reporter fella with the press card. I didn't make any of them sign the book, the way they all flooded in. Sorry I can't help you."

"That's okay," Nancy said. "Thanks anyway."

She glanced at her watch. She just had time to go home and get ready for her dinner date with David. She hoped he was having better luck with his inquiries than she was.

She took a quick shower, then changed into a dark blue skirt and light blue silky blouse. She

71

pulled back the sides of her strawberry blond hair into a Victorian silver hair clasp. The effect was just right for a place like the Riverside—not too formal, not too casual.

Bess's house was almost on the way to the restaurant. Nancy decided to stop and bring her friend up to date. She went up the steps and rang the bell.

When Bess opened the door, Nancy saw that her cheeks were stained with tears.

"Bess! What's wrong?" Nancy asked.

"You're what's wrong, you—you traitor!" Bess cried. "Go away! I never want to speak to you again!"

She slammed the door shut in Nancy's face.

Chapter

Eight

NANCY WAS TOO stunned to react. She and Bess had known each other since they were little, and for most of that time they had been the closest of friends. What could have happened to make Bess treat her like an enemy?

Nancy knew she had to find out what was wrong and fix it right then. The first step was to get Bess to listen to her.

Setting her jaw, Nancy put her finger on the doorbell and held it down.

Bing-bong! Bing-bong! Bing-bong!

After what seemed like dozens of rings, Nancy heard footsteps running toward the door. Just in time, too. Her finger was almost numb.

Bess flung open the door and cried, "Stop it! Why don't you go away and leave me alone!"

"Not until you tell me what's wrong," Nancy declared. "I have the right to expect at least that much from you."

Bess's stare was that of a puppy who had just been swatted with a newspaper. "What's wrong? How can you even ask? You know perfectly well what's wrong! Kyle called. He said that you think *he* killed Jack Broughton. He says you're hunting for evidence against him. Nancy, how could you! I asked you to help Kyle, not accuse him of murder!"

Nancy took a deep breath, which helped to calm her a little. "Did he tell you anything about his relationship with Broughton?" she asked.

"You mean the blackmail?" Bess replied. "Yes, he did. I'm glad. Now I understand what he's been going through the past couple of weeks."

"And you understand how someone could think that might be a motive for murder, don't you?" Nancy asked.

Bess shook her head. "I don't care. I *know* Kyle, and he could never kill anyone. Never! Besides, he told me he's innocent, and I believe him. I'm sorry, Nan, but unless you believe him, too, I can't go on being your friend."

Keeping her voice calm and sympathetic, Nancy said, "I'd like to believe him, Bess. I really would. But I can't shut my eyes to the facts. When the police find out that Broughton was blackmailing him and that he was nearby at the time of the murder, they're not going to care whether we believe him or not.

"The best way for us to prove that Kyle is innocent is to find the guilty person. And that is exactly what I'm trying to do. I could use your help, and even his, but with or without it, I'm going ahead."

Bess frowned. "According to the police, Broughton was killed by a burglar."

"That was yesterday. Today they think my father may have killed him." She quickly told Bess what had happened that day, not mentioning her suspicion that an anonymous tip from Kyle was what had motivated the police to suspect her father.

"But, Nancy, that's terrible! You must be a wreck," Bess exclaimed. "And your poor dad! What are you going to do?"

"I told you—find out who really killed Broughton," Nancy replied. "There must be other suspects. After all, blackmailers make a lot of enemies."

"That's true," Bess said, her face brightening. "All we have to do is find out who his other victims were. But how do we do that?"

Nancy noticed the significant *we*. "I'm guessing that Broughton's real reason for working at the firm was to dig up dirt on people," she said. "If I'm right, there must be clues in the files he consulted. That's where Kyle could help, by seeing which clients seem like possibilities. Then we can check them out."

"You're on," Bess declared. "I was planning to go shopping tomorrow, but I'd much rather help you—especially if it means we can help prove that Kyle's innocent."

Nancy didn't mention to Bess that their investigation might prove him guilty. If that happened, Bess would just have to deal with it, Nancy decided.

It crossed her mind then that if the police knew Kyle had been Broughton's blackmail victim, it would take some of the heat off her father. Washington would probably find it out sooner or later—but not from Nancy. She couldn't do that to Bess.

"Okay, I'll call you first thing tomorrow," Nancy said. Then she glanced at her watch. "Oh, rats! I'm supposed to meet David at the Riverside Restaurant in five minutes. I'll never get there on time!"

Bess gave her a sly look. "David? Who's David?" she asked. "Does Ned know about him?"

"This is a business conference," Nancy told her.

The drive to the restaurant took less time than Nancy expected. After parking the Mustang next to a purple van, she went inside. David hadn't arrived yet, but the headwaiter showed her to a table next to a window overlooking the Muskoka River and took away the Reserved card. While she waited, Nancy gazed out at the river and thought about Bess. She sincerely hoped that her friend was not about to face a terrible discovery about Kyle.

A pair of swans glided by lit by floodlights focused on the river. Nancy wasn't a bit superstitious, but she was tempted to take the pair of birds as a sign that the relationship between Bess and Kyle would work out.

"Nancy," David said, hurrying over to the table. "Sorry I'm late. I got a little lost on the way here."

He sat down and glanced out the window. "Too bad it's not warm enough to sit on the terrace," he added. "But this is almost as good as being outside. Did you notice the swans?" he added, pointing.

"They're beautiful, aren't they?" Nancy replied. "Oh, you hurt your hand."

He glanced down at a bleeding knuckle. "It's nothing," he said. "I haven't gotten used to all the knobs on the car I rented. There's one I always knock into."

"That's so irritating," Nancy said sympathetically. "What an unusual ring."

"Is it?" He slipped it off and passed it to her. "It's my college ring. I guess it is a little different from most."

Nancy examined it briefly. "Eliot College," she read. "I don't think I've heard of it. Where is it?"

"Just outside Seattle, Washington," David replied. "It's pretty small. Not many people know of it here, but I liked it. Listen, Nancy, not to change the subject, but I heard a rumor this afternoon that the police were going to search your home and your father's office. I'm telling you so you won't be too thrown by it, if it happens."

"Thanks," she said dryly, "but it's already happened. You seem to be pretty well plugged in to local rumors, especially for someone who hasn't been in town that long."

"It's one of the skills I had to pick up when I decided on investigative journalism," he explained. "But it's not all that hard, once you know how. Most people love to show how much they know, if you give them the opening. The trick is to figure out whose inside information is the genuine article. But that just comes down to a lot of careful cross-checking of sources."

"You're really involved in what you do, aren't you?" Nancy said. "What first drew you to it?"

He laughed. "I guess I like to know inside information as much as anybody," he said.

"Oops! Here comes the waiter. I think we'd better study our menus."

For appetizers, they both ordered shrimp cocktails. For his main course, David chose broiled rainbow trout, while Nancy decided on grilled salmon steak. As the waiter walked away, Nancy said, "We seem to be on the same wavelength this evening."

For a moment David looked startled, almost alarmed. Then he laughed it off by saying, "We're both in the mood for fish, if that's what you mean. It must come from spending our time fishing for information."

Nancy groaned at his pun, but she didn't try to top it.

"Nancy?" David continued in more serious tones. "I heard another rumor today that I think you should know about. It's the reason the police wanted to search your house and your dad's office. Oddly enough, it concerns the article I'm working on, too."

Nancy, remembering her last exchange with Brenda, said, "Is this the idiotic tale about my dad stealing from his elderly clients?"

David blinked in surprise. "Why—yes, it is. You've heard it already, then."

"I certainly have," she replied grimly. "And I want to put a stop to it, right away. A rumor like that could destroy my dad's practice."

"Yes, I can see why," David replied.

"Has your investigation turned up any evidence that old people really are being swindled?" she asked. "Or is it still in the rumor stage?"

He hesitated. "No hard evidence so far," he said. "But you know what they say. Where there's smoke—"

"Sometimes there's fire," Nancy said, breaking in. "And sometimes just a smoke screen. Do you have any idea who started these rumors about my father?"

"I got my information from a secretary at police headquarters," he replied. "I doubt she'll say where she got it from, but I'll ask."

Just then the waiter arrived with their shrimp cocktails.

"I'd really appreciate your trying," Nancy told him.

As they ate, David told her some wonderful anecdotes about people he had met. He seemed especially fond of two charming rascals whose West Coast real-estate scam he had exposed.

"What happened to them?" Nancy asked, intrigued.

"Oh, they went to jail. But they didn't hold it against me. One of them even promised me a great deal on a second home as soon as he got out!

"The trouble is," he concluded, "I can't afford to carry out many investigations like that. They take too long and pay too little. Papers and magazines are more generous to delivery people than they are to free-lance writers. This nursing home piece is just about to drain me. I've checked out leads in a handful of cities and still have lots more to follow up on.

"I guess I could take a staff position and get a regular paycheck," David said, "but then it would be the editor who decides what stories I work on, not me. To do the kind of work I want to do, I should be independently wealthy."

As if afraid he had become too gloomy, David changed the subject and quizzed Nancy about all the things she thought he should see and do while he was in River Heights. She was surprised at how easily he kept her talking. He made only an occasional comment or asked a question. She began to see why he was good at his job.

After dinner David walked Nancy to her car. When she turned to thank him and say good night, she sensed that he was about to put his arms around her and kiss her. This was definitely a complication she didn't need. She quickly stuck out her hand for him to shake and said, "Good night, David. I'll call you tomorrow. And do try to run down the source of that rumor."

He took her hand and held it just a little bit longer than necessary, then gave her a quirky smile. "I will," he promised. "Sleep tight."

He walked away as Nancy slid into her car. She turned the ignition key. For a moment nothing happened. Then all at once there was a piercing whistle, followed by a small explosion. A cloud of dense white smoke started to boil out from under the hood of the Mustang.

Chapter

Nine

THE INSTANT the whistling noise began Nancy had started to react. She switched off the ignition, hit the release button on her seat belt, and yanked at the door handle. As the door swung open, she was already diving out and rolling toward the rear of the car, away from the engine. She sprang to her feet and backed up.

David came running over. "Are you all right?" he demanded, stepping between her and the Mustang and putting his hands on her shoulders. "What happened?"

The gravel in the parking lot had skinned Nancy's palms. She stepped back from David and tucked each of her hands under the opposite arm and pressed hard. That helped a little to ease the pain.

"I'm okay," she said breathlessly. "But my car—"

Over David's shoulder she could see that the cloud of white smoke was almost extinguished. One of the cooks, in white apron and high white chef's hat, had come running carrying a bright red fire extinguisher. Behind him, other members of the restaurant staff had stepped outside to watch or help.

Nancy went to meet him and said, "It's all right, thanks. I think it was just somebody's idea of a practical joke."

"Are you sure, miss?" he asked in a faint European accent. "A car fire is no joke. I had a Fiat once—"

"I'm sure," Nancy said, breaking in on his story. "But thanks again."

He seemed almost disappointed to be robbed of his chance to be a hero. As the cook returned to the kitchen, David joined Nancy. "A joke?" he said. "How do you know? I think we should call a garage to come get your car."

"I doubt if that's necessary," Nancy replied. "Someone wired one of these so-called car bombs to a friend's car last year. They're pretty startling, but they don't do any real damage to a car.

"I should check just the same," she added, going back to the car and leaning in to pull the hood latch. "But I'm almost positive that's what it is."

When the hood popped open, the smell reminded Nancy of Fourth of July picnics minus the hot dogs and burgers.

David pulled a small flashlight from his pocket. "There it is," he said, aiming the light at a blackened cardboard tube that dangled from the distributor. He leaned over and detached the thin wires, then studied it. "I guess when you turn on the ignition, the current sets it off. Cute."

"I'll take that," Nancy said, reaching for the car bomb. "It could be a clue."

"Oh, sorry," David said. "I got my fingerprints all over it."

Nancy borrowed his light and shone it around the engine compartment, then closed the hood. "It looks okay," she reported.

David frowned. "I don't like the feel of this. It could just as easily have been a real bomb. I wonder if you ought to drop out of this investigation."

"Sorry," Nancy said. "There's no way I'm going to allow myself to be scared off. Too much is at stake—such as my father's reputation."

David nodded as if he had expected her answer. "Would you like me to try starting the engine for you?" he asked.

"Thanks, but I'll do it," Nancy replied. "I doubt if I'll have any more trouble."

"Okay, but if you don't mind, I'll follow you home. Just in case that gizmo caused some problems that don't show up until you're on your way." He waited while Nancy got the engine going and backed out of her parking place. Then he returned to his own car and pulled in behind her.

Nancy's mind was focused half on her driving and half on what had just happened. The car bomb was not a random prank, she was sure of that. It had been aimed *at her,* as a warning. But by whom? Broughton's killer was the obvious candidate, but how had he known where to find her car? She didn't think anyone had been following her, but then, too, she had to admit that she hadn't been watching.

Her heart sank. She had told Bess that she was on her way to dinner and had named the Riverside Restaurant. What if Bess casually mentioned that fact to Kyle? He could have easily installed the prank bomb while Nancy and David were having dinner.

After reaching her street, she pulled into the driveway. Behind her, David lightly tapped his horn before driving off. As she walked to the door, Nancy thought about the evening as a whole.

Except for the moment when her car seemed about to blow up, she had thoroughly enjoyed her date with David. She had to admit that *date* was a better word than *conference,* whatever she might have said to Bess. David was clearly attracted to her, and she— How *did* she feel about him?

She admired his devotion to his craft, which had much in common with her own detective work. Also he was good-looking and fun to be with, but, she knew, he was no threat to her relationship with Ned. That was different—not a casual flirtation, but real, true love. If only Ned weren't away at college!

She sat down at her desk and wrote Ned a quick note, telling him how much she missed him. She could fill him in on her current investigation—and David Megali—the next time she saw him.

At breakfast the next morning Carson Drew was somber. "The police don't have a bit of evidence against me," he said. "Not that that will stop them from suspecting me."

He took a sip of his coffee, then added, "But the police investigation isn't my biggest concern. I'm still having trouble taking in Jack's death. And then there's the publicity. First someone on my staff is murdered in the office, then rumors appear to suggest that I'm responsible. It's getting in the way of maintaining my clients' confidence in my integrity.

"To give you one example, my client in that

product liability case asked me about Jack yesterday afternoon. The message from him was that these suspicions could undermine my ability to function as his counsel."

"It'll be all right, Dad," Nancy said, patting his hand. "I'll get to the bottom of this, and once the real killer is unmasked, everyone will realize how badly you've been treated."

Carson shook his head slowly. "I'm not sure it's wise for you to go on with this case, Nancy," he said. "You can't possibly be impartial—not with me on the short list of suspects. And whatever you uncover, most people are bound to think that you're simply trying to exonerate me."

"If I paid attention to what 'some people' think, I'd never solve any of my cases," Nancy retorted. "Don't worry, Dad—I'll be careful. But I'm not giving up!"

Before leaving the house, Nancy telephoned Bess and arranged to meet her at Carson Drew's office. When Nancy arrived, she found Bess already in the reception area, looking at a magazine.

"Oh, Nancy," Bess said, speaking in an undertone. "I told Kyle your idea about the files last night. He was so excited that he wanted to get started checking them first thing this morning. He even took me home early."

Nancy smiled, but inwardly she wondered if Kyle had ended his date with Bess early to give himself time to wire the smoke bomb to Nancy's car.

"Oh, look. There he is," Bess said, pointing down the hall. "Kyle! Yoo-hoo, Kyle!"

Carla was aghast. *No one* shouted "Yoo-hoo!" in the reception room.

Nancy quickly took Bess's arm and led her down the hall to where Kyle was standing loaded down with file folders.

"Hi, Bess. Hi, Nancy," he said. "I think I may be getting somewhere. Let me show you."

They followed him into Broughton's former office. Kyle dumped the files on the desk and picked up a notepad.

"Jack checked out dozens and dozens of the firm's files," he explained. "That was his job, after all—to reorganize and computerize the filing system. But if Nancy's right, he was also searching for victims for his blackmail racket."

Bess groaned at the size of the pile of folders. "It'll take forever to look through all of these, and even then we might miss something important."

Kyle nodded. "I know. But then it came to me. Ms. Hildebrand's log shows the date and time each file was checked out and returned. Usually Jack checked out eight or ten at once and returned them all at the same time. But when I looked more carefully, I saw that there were a few files he kept longer. And there was one that he checked out not once, but *three times.*"

Nancy began to feel the first tremors of excitement. "Whose file is it?" she demanded.

"It's a divorce case," Kyle replied. "A very messy one, too. Our client is the husband, and if some of the information in the file got into the hands of his wife's attorneys, it would probably cost him a whole lot of money."

"And you think that Broughton may have tried to extort money from the husband as his price for not passing this information on?"

"Maybe. Or he may have tried to sell the information to the wife's attorneys and the husband found out about it," Kyle replied.

"Who is he?" Bess asked, thrilled. "We have to question him!"

"His name's Al Fortunato," Kyle replied. "He owns a junkyard and tow truck business. It's over on the south side, near the town line."

Nancy frowned. Kyle's report reminded her of something, but what? The harder she tried to pin it down, the farther it slipped away.

Then all at once she had it! The slip of paper she had found in Broughton's jacket. She had rightly deciphered "KY D" to mean Kyle Donovan and "100/WK?" as the amount Broughton was demanding from Kyle. But what about the line above that—"DAM ALF SG"? "ALF" could stand for Al Fortunato!

"Do you know anything more about Fortunato?" Nancy asked.

Kyle shrugged. "I saw him here a couple of times, when he came in for appointments. He's a big, burly guy who looks like he's been in a fight or two in his day. Running a junkyard must be a lot rougher than operating a tearoom."

"Nancy, let's go see him!" Bess exclaimed. "Right away!"

"All right," Nancy agreed. Kyle's reasoning about the files impressed her, and the note she'd found in Broughton's own handwriting seemed to corroborate his suspicions. The junkyard owner definitely had to be checked out, and the sooner the better. Still, she reminded herself, even if Fortunato turned out to be one of Broughton's blackmail victims, he wasn't necessarily Broughton's murderer.

Before she and Bess left the office, Nancy called David's number. He wasn't in, but she left a message on his machine, asking if he had any information about Al Fortunato. She promised to call back later.

Fortunato's wrecking yard was on a busy stretch of Henderson Road between a tire dealership and a frozen yogurt stand. A line of tall, thick hedges hid the yard from the road. Nancy spotted it by the four tow trucks parked out front and the billboard-size sign that said Fortune Salvage—Car Parts All Model Years. She parked near the tow trucks.

Inside the yard Nancy and Bess saw stacks of

junked cars, three and four high, that stretched in every direction. To her left Nancy noticed a pile of car doors, each carefully marked with the make, year, and model. Next to it was a stack of windshields separated by lengths of lumber.

A dozen feet away a heavyset man with close-cropped hair and a nose that bent to one side was talking to two younger men in oil-stained overalls. He noticed Nancy and Bess and called out, "You girls need something?"

"Mr. Fortunato?" Nancy said.

"That's me," he said. "What about it?"

"I'm Nancy Drew. Could we talk to you for a couple of minutes?"

"Drew," he repeated. "Carson Drew's kid? Sure, soon as I'm done here. You can wait in the office if you want."

He waved in the direction of a rusty mobile home. Nancy and Bess walked over to it and went inside. The main room was furnished with a battered desk, two metal file cabinets, several folding chairs, and a computer and fax machine.

"He doesn't believe in putting on airs, does he?" Bess said, giggling.

Nancy studied the file cabinets. The drawers of one were labeled Catalogs, Manuals, Invoices, and Misc Junk. The other had labels for A–G, H–M, N–S, and T–Z.

"Watch the door," Nancy told Bess, and pulled open the A–G drawer.

She quickly located the *B*'s and started flipping through the tabs on the files. She was just passing the one for Branford Motors when a loud, angry voice rang out, "Hey! What do you think you're doing?"

Chapter

Ten

Nancy hurriedly slid the file drawer closed, taking care to avoid banging it. Putting on the most innocent expression she could manage, she turned—to see that she and Bess were still alone in the room.

"Sorry, Al," a second voice said. It too sounded close at hand. Nancy noticed that the window of the trailer was propped open. "I thought you'd want me to tow it in," the voice continued. "Some turkey took off the plates and left it parked half up on the pavement."

Nancy gave a heartfelt sigh of relief and went over to the window. Fortunato was just a few feet away, talking to a tow truck driver. "Okay, okay," he said. "It's good for nothing but scrap, but stick it in Aisle Eight for now."

The tow truck pulled away in a haze of diesel fumes, and Fortunato came into the trailer. He took up a lot of space. "So, what can I do for you?" he asked Nancy.

"You probably heard about what happened at my dad's office," Nancy began.

"Sure, there was a story on TV," Fortunato replied. "So what? The robber didn't make off with anything of mine, did he?"

"As far as we know, he didn't take anything," Nancy assured him.

Fortunato relaxed a little. "Oh," he said. "Then why the personal visit from the boss's daughter?"

Nancy tried to keep her tone casual. "Mr. Fortunato, did you have any contact with Jack Broughton, the man who was killed?"

Fortunato's face became hard and mean. "I got nothing to say about that," he growled. "No, I take that back. I got one thing to say. Broughton was scum, and whoever gave him the ax did the world a favor. Anything else? I'm a busy man."

Nancy looked over at Bess, who motioned toward the door with her head. Nancy nodded. "Thanks for your time," she said to Fortunato, and followed Bess outside.

They were silent until they reached Nancy's car, then Bess said, "Well! If that wasn't guilt, I don't know what was!"

"Anger, maybe," Nancy replied. "It's clear to

me that Fortunato *did* know Broughton. Whether or not he was being blackmailed by him I couldn't tell, but he obviously never felt friendly toward Broughton."

She started the car and drove a quarter of a mile to the nearest pay phone. "I'll just be a minute," she promised Bess.

It took over five minutes just to get through to Chief McGinnis of the River Heights Police Department.

"Hello, Nancy," he said. "How are you and your dad holding up?"

"As well as can be expected," Nancy replied. "It's not easy, hearing all these terrible rumors about my dad and seeing that the River Heights Police Department is taking them seriously."

"I'm really sorry," the chief said. "Ron Washington is a fine cop, but he's new to our force and doesn't really know your dad. It's his investigation, and I have to let him run it as he sees fit."

"Dad and I both understand, Chief," Nancy assured him. "And don't worry—I'm not calling to ask for any special treatment. But I would like a small favor. Would you see if you have anything about an Al Fortunato on your computer?"

Nancy was relieved when the chief agreed to help. When she finally returned to the car, she was grinning.

"Well?" Bess demanded.

"Al Fortunato was arrested four times in the

last six years, each time for assault," Nancy reported. "But the charges were dropped three times. The fourth time, he plea-bargained it down to disorderly conduct and paid a fine. My dad was his lawyer, by the way."

"So Fortunato has a history of violence," Bess mused. "If Broughton *was* trying to blackmail him, Fortunato is the kind of guy who might have snapped and killed him, without meaning to."

"Could be," Nancy said. "But all we have is a potential motive with no hard evidence to back it up. And we don't have any witnesses who can place Fortunato at the scene."

Bess grimaced. "Do you always have to be so *logical?*" she demanded plaintively. "I think it comes from not eating enough. Why don't we call Kyle and see if he's free to meet us for lunch?"

"Detective work really builds an appetite, doesn't it?" Nancy replied with a laugh. "Okay, give him a call. Do you need change?"

Bess got out and went to the pay phone. A couple of minutes later she returned to the car with a dreamy smile on her face. Nancy's heart sank as she thought about what it would do to Bess if Kyle turned out to be the murderer.

"Kyle would love to have lunch with us," Bess reported. "Do you know the Four Brothers Diner? He'll meet us there in fifteen minutes."

Nancy remembered the Four Brothers. It was an old-fashioned diner shaped like a railway car, with shiny metal sides and a big neon sign that said Eats. She drove to it and parked near the entrance. Kyle wasn't there yet, but she and Bess went in and claimed a booth. While Nancy studied the menu, Bess scanned the jukebox.

"Fabulous!" she exclaimed. "They've got every fifties and sixties hit I ever heard of, and a lot I don't know. Nancy, I think we wandered into a time warp!"

"The prices are behind the times, too," Nancy observed. "I'm going to have to come here more often. Oh—there's Kyle."

Bess waved out the window, then sat back with a contented smile. "Don't you just love the way he walks?" she demanded.

"First one leg, then the other, you mean?" Nancy retorted. "Very original."

"You!" Bess said, making a face. "What do you know about new love? You and Ned have been going together for ages. But this—this is new and wonderful!"

Nancy had just enough time to say "I'll take your word for it." Then Kyle was standing next to the booth, giving Bess a big smile. Nancy received a slightly smaller one.

"Have you ordered yet?" Kyle asked, slipping into the booth next to Bess.

"We were waiting for you," Bess said, beaming.

The waitress came over and took their order,

then turned and shouted it into the kitchen in true diner fashion. As she walked away, Kyle asked, "Did you learn anything at Fortunato's place?"

"A little," Nancy replied. "He obviously had had some contact with Broughton, and he didn't like it, or him. And he seems to be the kind of guy who might throw a punch when he gets upset."

"He seemed a little scary to me," Bess added.

Kyle frowned. "Wait a minute," he said, slapping his forehead. "I just remembered something about the night Broughton was killed and I was hanging around on the street downstairs. When I walked past the coffee shop one time, I peeked in and saw someone who looked familiar. I realize now it was Fortunato!"

"Kyle, you're wonderful!" Bess exclaimed. "That means we can place him at the scene of the crime. He's obviously the murderer! We should tell the detective who's in charge of the case right away and have him arrest Fortunato."

"Not quite so fast," Nancy said grimly. "If Kyle tells the police about seeing Fortunato, he's also placing himself on the scene. The police might think that Kyle's motive is at least as strong as Fortunato's and arrest him instead."

She didn't say it out loud, but she thought that this sudden recollection of Kyle's was also very conveniently timed.

Bess's face fell. "Oh," she said. "I hadn't

thought of that. I guess you're right. Maybe we shouldn't tell the police yet. But at least we know to watch Fortunato."

At that point the waitress arrived with their sandwiches and sodas. "Anyone want my pickle?" Bess asked. Nancy declined. So did Kyle.

Nancy's BLT was just the way she liked it—crisp bacon, crunchy lettuce, and ripe, juicy tomato slices on toast that was exactly the right shade of brown.

"What next?" Bess asked as she was finishing her hamburger.

The waitress arrived right then and said, "Any desserts? You should try the banana cream pie. We make it ourselves."

Bess's eyes grew wider. "I really shouldn't," she said in a tone that made it clear she was going to.

"Why don't we share a piece?" Kyle said, putting an arm around Bess's shoulders for a moment. "One piece of banana cream pie and two forks, please."

The waitress gave Nancy a questioning look.

"I'll have chocolate pudding," Nancy said. "No whipped cream." To Bess and Kyle, she said, "I'll be right back. I want to make a call."

The pay phone was at the far end of the counter, near the door to the rest rooms. As she approached it, Nancy spotted an Out of Order sign taped to the coin slot.

"You need a phone?" the waitress called. "That one's broken, but there's a booth outside at the corner of the parking lot."

"Thanks," Nancy called back, and changed course for the door.

The telephone was inside a metal and glass booth with a folding door. There was a lot of noise from the traffic, but once Nancy slid the door closed it faded. She put in her coins and dialed David's number. Four rings, then his machine answered.

She waited out the message, then said, "Hi, David, this is Nancy." She was about to ask him to call her at her father's office when she was distracted by a sudden squeal of tires. She peeked back over her shoulder and saw that a beat-up blue sedan had just sped into the diner parking lot. It was going much too fast, straight toward a row of parked cars. Just when Nancy was sure that it was about to crash, the driver swerved. The car went into a skid and began to slide sideways, heading straight for the phone booth.

Horrified, Nancy grabbed the door handle and pulled, but nothing moved. The folding door was stuck. She couldn't get out!

Chapter

Eleven

FRANTICALLY NANCY jiggled the door, but there was no time. The car was going to crash into the phone booth and flatten her!

Then Nancy remembered the hard plastic receiver in her right hand. She lifted it high over her head and slammed it against the glass with every ounce of force she could summon. An eight-pointed star appeared in the safety glass, but it didn't shatter.

"Come on!" she muttered through clenched teeth. "*Break!*"

Again she struck the glass. Finally it collapsed in a shower of small greenish transparent pebbles that glistened in the sunlight. Before the last of them had tinkled to the ground, Nancy dove through the opening and rolled away from the booth.

At the last moment the driver of the battered car seemed to regain control over it. It came out of the skid just two feet from the phone booth and started to move forward in the direction of the street. As it passed the phone booth, it fishtailed and the back fender struck the booth. The booth stayed upright, but the other panes of glass shattered.

Nancy got to her hands and knees as the blue sedan reached the street and darted in front of an oncoming car. As horns blared, Nancy had just enough time to notice that the license plate on the sedan was covered with dried mud, and the driver's face was hidden by a ski mask.

As Nancy stood up and brushed herself off, Bess and Kyle came running from the diner.

"Nancy, what happened?" Bess cried.

Nancy stared at the remains of the phone booth. "That phone booth was just wrecked," she said ruefully. "And I was almost wrecked with it!"

"People like that shouldn't be allowed on the road," Kyle declared. "It's criminal!"

"That's truer than you think," Nancy replied. "What just happened was no accident. The driver was wearing a mask. The question is, was his attack meant to scare me off or to get me out of the way for good?"

"Nancy! That car!" Bess exclaimed. "There

must have been half a dozen like it at Fortunato's wrecking yard. I bet he followed us here!"

This thought had occurred to Nancy, too. Would a criminal choose a weapon that pointed so obviously to himself? He might, if he expected his crime to be taken for an accident.

Something else also occurred to Nancy. At the moment that the blue car was skidding in her direction, Kyle Donovan was inside the diner with Bess. That meant that unless he had an accomplice, Kyle was probably in the clear.

"With all this excitement, I totally lost track of the time," Kyle suddenly said. "I've got to get back to the office."

"We're on our way there, too," Nancy said.

"We are?" Bess said in surprise. "Oh, okay." As they walked back across the parking lot, she added, "Since we're all going the same way, I think I'll ride with Kyle. That's okay with you, isn't it, Nancy?"

"Sure," Nancy replied. As she said it, she realized that she had been looking forward to the drive downtown as a time to discuss what had just happened with Bess. Now Kyle was taking that time away from her. Well, she would simply have to talk to herself about the case!

The clues pointed pretty clearly toward Fortunato as being the guilty party. The person who staged the attack on her just now *had* to have known where to find her. She couldn't be absolutely positive, but she didn't believe anyone had been tailing her all morning. Fortunato could have followed her the mile or so from his place to the diner without her catching on, and he certainly had easy access to plenty of old, nondescript cars.

Nancy parked in the lot behind the office building and took the elevator up. As the doors opened on her father's floor, she reminded herself that she still couldn't exclude a killer from Broughton's past in another town. If so, she was going to have a very hard time tracking that person down.

Nancy went to Broughton's office, sat down at his desk, and pulled the telephone closer. The envelope with Broughton's résumé was still in her purse. She glanced through it, looking for the section on employment history. Once she found it, she decided to work backward from his last job at a law firm in Omaha, Nebraska.

Her call was answered on the first ring. "Backman, Turner, good morning," the receptionist said.

Nancy quickly explained who she was and asked to speak to someone who could verify Jack Broughton's references. She didn't mention that Broughton was dead.

A moment later a woman came on the line. "This is Alice Turner," she said. "May I help you?"

Nancy explained once again. There was a long silence. Then Ms. Turner said, "I would much prefer not to be a character reference for Mr. Broughton."

"May I ask why not?" Nancy replied.

Another long silence, then Ms. Turner said, very slowly, as if choosing her words with care, "I have no wish to slander anyone. Let me just say that I would hesitate to entrust sensitive, confidential information about my clients to anyone whose honesty or discretion I had any reason to doubt. Now if you'll excuse me, I have a call on another line."

Well! Nancy thought as she replaced the receiver. That was about as close to an accusation as a cautious attorney was likely to make. Apparently Broughton's career as a blackmailer had started before he came to River Heights. How much before? And why had he been hired at her father's firm with such a bad reference?

Nancy was about to place a call to Broughton's previous employer, in Billings, Montana, when Kyle and Bess came in. Kyle was carrying three thick files.

"These are the other files that Jack kept out longer than usual," Kyle reported. "Bess and I thought we should go through them together."

"Good idea," Nancy replied. "Whose are they?"

Kyle put the stack on the desk and opened the top one. He scanned a couple of pages, then said, "This one's a start-up software company that's planning to go public early next year. That's always a sensitive time for a new company. Any negative information can cost the founders a lot of money."

"Do you think that's what Broughton was looking for?" Bess asked.

Kyle shrugged. "Maybe. But there's nothing to show that he found any."

The second file was that of a local surgeon whose wife had died, leaving him with two small children. Most of the documents concerned trust funds. Kyle thumbed through them, then said, "I don't see anything out of line here, either. I suspect Jack was simply fishing, hoping to hook a big one."

He opened the last of the files. "Winona Carlisle," he read. "In care of Crestwood Manor."

"That's that very ritzy nursing home out near the country club," Bess remarked.

Nursing home? Nancy's ears pricked up. Someone, probably Broughton or his killer, had promised David Megali some information about elderly clients in nursing homes. Someone, almost certainly the killer, had tipped off both the police and the press that Carson Drew was stealing from his elderly clients.

"Here, let me see that," Nancy said, reaching for the file. She flipped through the pages. Winona Carlisle was apparently a very wealthy woman who owned several office buildings. The file also contained a list of substantial contributions to local and national wildlife organizations. There were check marks and percentages next to the names of some of the organizations, with a note at the bottom, "For will."

Nancy showed it to Kyle. "That probably means Mrs. Carlisle's will, right?"

"That'd be my guess," Kyle replied. "But you can check easily enough. If the firm drafted her will, there should be a copy in the file. The original wills—the ones that have been signed and witnessed—are kept in the vault."

Nancy went through the file quickly, then again, more carefully. "No will," she said. She picked up the phone and dialed her father's extension, but there was no answer. She tried Margaret Hildebrand. "Do you know if the firm is holding a will for someone named Winona Carlisle?" she asked.

"I'd have to check," the firm's librarian admitted. "Would you like me to find out? I can call you back."

Five minutes later Margaret appeared in the

office doorway, obviously very upset. "I don't know what Mr. Drew is going to say," she began. "This has never happened before."

"What?" Nancy asked, though she could already guess the answer.

"The last will and testament of Winona Carlisle *should* be on file here," Margaret said. "But I just checked in the vault, and it isn't where it ought to be. It may have been misfiled—I'm going through the whole drawer again—but I thought you ought to know right away."

"Thanks," Nancy said. "You'll be sure to tell my dad when he returns?"

The librarian nodded her head. "I sure will. He's going to be very unhappy when he hears."

"So," Kyle said after Ms. Hildebrand left. "The vault *was* broken into the night Jack was killed. He really did surprise a burglar, just as the police said."

Nancy frowned. "Not so fast," she said. "It could be that the burglar, if there was one, was after one specific thing—Winona Carlisle's will. And we know Broughton took a special interest in her *and* that the copy of her will is missing from her file. He could easily have taken it, *and* the signed will from the vault, then faked the burglary to cover his tracks. The question is, why? Was he extorting money from Mrs. Carlisle, or planning to?"

"I still think Fortunato's the murderer," Bess declared. "Why else was he hanging around the night of the murder? And what about that car that nearly ran you down? You don't really believe it was being driven by a little old lady, do you?"

"No," Nancy said, laughing. "But I can ask her when I see her." She phoned the nursing home and learned that visitors were permitted that afternoon, beginning in half an hour.

"Do you want me to come along?" Bess asked.

"I don't think so," Nancy replied. "We might have trouble getting more than one person in to see her, and a crowd might make her nervous."

"Okay, then I'm going to run a few errands," Bess said. "Kyle, as soon as you can get away from the office, why don't we take another look at Fortunato's wrecking yard? I'm *sure* he's hiding something."

Crestwood Manor was a former private mansion set amid acres of lawns and gardens. Nancy parked and went in the front door. When she told the man at the desk that she was the daughter of Mrs. Carlisle's attorney, he telephoned, then said that Mrs. Carlisle would meet her in the solarium.

Nancy followed his directions to a room with many tall windows and cheerful wicker furniture.

Mrs. Carlisle, a short, plump woman with thin-ning white hair and cool, shrewd eyes, was al-ready there, seated in a wicker armchair. She was grasping a slender wooden cane with a silver head in the form of a bird.

"You're Carson Drew's daughter, are you?" she began. "I suppose he's too busy to come speak to me himself. Well, girl, what is it? What do you want?"

"I understand my dad's firm drafted your will," Nancy said.

The woman's eyes narrowed. "Of course they did," she snapped. "And charged handsomely for the job, too! What of it?"

"Do you know where that will is now?"

"Don't *you* know?" Mrs. Carlisle asked. "It's supposed to be with my other papers at your daddy's office. Are you trying to tell me that it's not there?"

"Well . . ."

The woman banged her cane on the floor. Her voice rose, nearly to a shout. "They got to you, didn't they? They still think they're going to lay their filthy murdering hands on my money! Well, I may be an old woman, but I still have a few surprises for them!"

"Mrs. Carlisle," Nancy started to say, "I just—"

"And for you and your father, too!" Mrs.

Carlisle pushed herself up out of the chair and tottered on her feet. Thinking she was about to fall, Nancy took a step toward her. Just then, the elderly woman raised her cane in the air and brought it down toward Nancy's head.

Chapter
Twelve

NANCY THREW HERSELF to the right as the cane whistled toward her. It missed, but Nancy felt the breeze as the cane went by. An instant later it crashed against the arm of the wicker chair.

As Mrs. Carlisle raised the cane for another try, Nancy backed toward the door. Before she got there, it opened and a man came in.

"Is there a problem here?" he asked, going up to Mrs. Carlisle.

"Charles! Throw this young woman out— right now! And don't let her come back!"

"You shouldn't excite yourself, Mrs. Carlisle," Charles murmured. "Would you like me to call down for a cup of herb tea?"

"Get her out of here!" She pointed her cane at the door, narrowly missing his head.

Charles turned to Nancy. "I'm sorry, miss," he said politely but firmly, "I'm afraid you'd better leave. This way, please."

As she followed him into the front hall, Nancy said, "I'm sorry I upset her. I didn't mean to. Maybe if I came back another time—"

"I'm afraid that won't be possible," Charles said. He opened the front door and held it for her. "Our guests expect us to protect them from unwelcome visitors. If either you or your associate return, I'll be forced to have you arrested for trespassing."

"Associate?" Nancy said, turning back. "But I don't—"

She found that she was talking to a closed door. She knocked and rang the buzzer, but there was no response. Finally she gave up and went to her car. As she drove back downtown, she thought what a shame it was that Mrs. Carlisle had been so badly upset. Still, she *had* learned two important facts. First, Mrs. Carlisle was convinced that someone was after her money. And second, somebody else had recently shown an interest in the elderly woman. Nancy had a hunch that that somebody was involved in Broughton's murder. How to track him down? That was the problem.

"Oh, Nancy!" Carla said when Nancy walked into the law firm's reception area. "Your father asked me to make sure that you see him the moment you got back."

When Nancy pushed open the door to her father's office, she saw him sitting with his head in his hands. He lowered his hands and raised his eyes. She had never seen his face so drawn.

"The buzzards are circling," he said. He tried to smile to take the edge off his comment, but the effort defeated him. He picked up a stack of pink message slips. "These are all from newspaper and TV reporters who want to interview me. I don't think they're calling to find out my views about the latest Supreme Court decision."

The telephone buzzed. He picked it up, listened for a moment, then replaced it. "The police," he said, rubbing his eyes. "They asked to see me again tomorrow morning at headquarters. At least they're still asking."

"Don't worry, Dad," Nancy said. She circled the desk and gave him a quick hug. "We're a lot closer to solving this business."

"I heard," he said. "A missing will, eh? I wonder what the connection is to Broughton's death. Was there really a burglar after all?"

Nancy quickly explained why that didn't seem likely, then asked, "Do you remember anything about Mrs. Carlisle's will?"

Carson shook his head. "I'm not even sure that I drafted it," he said. "She was never a big client of the firm. I doubt if I met her more than two or three times over the years. I have a vague feeling that she planned to leave the bulk of her estate to various causes—birds, perhaps? Something like that."

"Suppose we hadn't discovered that the will was missing?" Nancy asked. "What would have happened when she passed on?"

"We would have hunted for the will and not found it," Carson replied. "In that case, the laws are very clear. The estate would go to her nearest living relative, whoever that might be."

"I didn't see any mention of relatives in her file," Nancy observed.

"She may not have any. If none come forward, after a waiting period, the state takes over the property—unless, of course, someone can prove to the court that she intended to leave it to him or her."

"I just *know* that Mrs. Carlisle is the key to this," Nancy declared. "But how? Did Broughton steal her will? Or was it his killer? And in either case, why? Are you sure you can't tell me anything more about her?"

Carson raised his palms in a gesture of helplessness. "I'm sorry, Nancy," he said. "As I told you, I doubt if I met the lady more than two or three times. I know she had the reputation of being a very shrewd businesswoman, and I seem to recall some story about a tragedy in her past, but that's it."

Suddenly alert, Nancy asked, "What sort of tragedy?"

"An accident of some sort. I don't recall."

"Hmm—I wonder if whatever it was made the newspapers?" Nancy mused.

She was about to ask about Jack Broughton's job references when there was a tap on the door. Ms. Hanson put her head in. "Oh, Nancy," she said. "There's a call for you on three from a David Megali."

"Finally!" Nancy said. "Thanks, Ms. Hanson. Can I take it at your desk? Dad, I'll catch you later."

She hurried out and picked up the phone. "Hi, Nancy," David said. "I got your messages today, but I've been running around like crazy."

"That's okay," Nancy replied. "How did you track me down?"

He laughed. "I called your house, and the woman I spoke to told me to try your father's office. Simple, huh? So, have you found out anything new?"

"I certainly have," Nancy replied. "And it may tie in to your investigation, too."

She told him a little about Mrs. Carlisle, though she didn't mention the missing will. When she finished, he said, "Crestwood Manor?

I've heard of it, of course. Very upscale, very comfortable. And very profitable, too, I bet. But none of my sources has mentioned it in connection with the kind of abuses I'm researching. I don't recall the name Carlisle, either."

"Oh. Too bad," Nancy said. The disappointment she felt took her by surprise. Had she really expected David to solve the case for her?

"I couldn't get anything more on who spread the rumors about your father," David continued. "I have gathered a lot of other information. Some of it may help you solve your case. Why don't we meet for dinner? I'll lay it all out for you."

Nancy's spirits lifted. "Great," she said. "But not at the Riverside. I really enjoyed our meal there, but it gave my car indigestion."

He laughed. "Okay, then, I noticed a Middle Eastern restaurant not far from downtown," he said. "How does seven o'clock sound?"

Nancy hesitated. "Can we make it a bit later?" she asked. "I need to go by the library first. I thought I might find some background information on Winona Carlisle in the newspaper files."

"Sure, no problem," David replied. They agreed on the place for eight o'clock and hung up.

After the call from David, Nancy found herself oddly troubled. She tried to calm down by checking over her notes on the case, but it didn't work. She kept finding herself staring blankly into space.

It was time for drastic measures. She reached for the telephone and dialed Ned Nickerson's number. The rush of happiness she felt when he answered told her that this was the right prescription for what was bothering her.

"Hi, Nancy," Ned said. "I was going to call you tonight. What's all this about somebody being killed in your father's office? I saw a story on the news last night. Are you on the case?"

"Yes. I tried to call you earlier, but it's been hectic around here," Nancy said. She quickly filled him in on her investigation. Each time she mentioned David's name she sensed herself stumbling a little. Ned apparently noticed.

"Tell me again who this guy David is," he said when she finished. "He's a reporter? For what paper?"

"He's not a reporter, he's a free-lance journalist," Nancy replied. "He's written for a lot of important magazines."

"Yeah? That's nice," Ned said dryly. "River Heights must really feel like the sticks to him, then. How long is he planning to hang around?"

Nancy hesitated. It hadn't sunk in that David was in town for just a limited time. "I don't know—until he collects the information he needs for his article, I guess. Why?"

"I was wondering how many more dinners you're planning to have with him," Ned said. "Tonight'll make two in a row."

"Why, Nickerson, I think you're jealous!" Nancy said with a giggle. "You should know better. You're the one I love. But David *is* an experienced investigator, and I think he can help me with this case. And he *is* pretty cute," she added, teasing Ned.

"He'd better keep his distance, or he won't be so cute when I'm done with him," Ned growled. "You take care of yourself, do you hear? Someone out there is a killer, and he's already made at least one try for you."

"I'll be careful," Nancy promised. She was about to say more when the telephone buzzed. "Hold on a sec," she said, and pressed the intercom button.

"Is that Nancy?" Carla said. "You've got a call on two. She said it's urgent."

Nancy switched back to Ned and told him goodbye, then pressed the blinking button for the other line and said, "Hello?"

"Nancy?" Bess said urgently. "Listen, we're at the junkyard—I mean near the junkyard, down the street—and I think we've spotted the car that tried to run you over today at the diner. You've got to come over here—right away!"

Chapter
Thirteen

As NANCY DROVE out Henderson Road toward Al Fortunato's wrecking yard, she asked herself why she wasn't more excited about the discovery Bess and Kyle had apparently made. Was it because she didn't *want* Fortunato to be the killer? Or simply that the net of clues was drawing tighter, and she didn't think Fortunato was secured yet?

As arranged, Bess and Kyle were waiting in Bess's car in the parking lot of the frozen yogurt stand next to the wrecking yard. Nancy pulled in alongside them, got out, and went over to order a double cone, vanilla and strawberry. She wasn't really hungry, but her sense of fairness told her that if they made use of the parking lot, they ought to buy something. When her cone came, she carried it over to Bess's car and got in.

"I'm *sure* it's the same car," Bess said, almost bouncing up and down on the seat. "We almost missed it because it's partly hidden behind the office trailer. That's suspicious right there, if you ask me. Why hide a dumb old car unless you're afraid somebody might see it?"

"What we call hiding it somebody else might call just getting it out of the way," Kyle pointed out in a let's-look-at-both-sides-of-the-question tone of voice. "We don't *know* it's the same car, and even if it is, what real evidence do we have to link it to Fortunato?"

"It's in his yard, isn't it?" Bess retorted impatiently. "That's a link. And we're not going to find out if it's the same car by sitting here, yakking and eating yogurt. We have to go check it out."

"Fortunato won't be very happy to see us again," Nancy said.

"What if I go in first?" Kyle offered. "If he's there, I'll start asking him a lot of questions about carburetors or something. He doesn't know me, so he won't suspect anything. And while he's talking to me, you two can slip past and check out the car."

"Good plan," Nancy said.

They walked down the road to the big Fortune Salvage sign. Nancy and Bess waited, out of sight, while Kyle strolled into the wrecking yard. Through the hedge, Nancy could just glimpse him standing with another person who had to be Fortunato. Kyle gestured, and the two of them walked off to the left.

"Now!" Nancy muttered. She and Bess ran into the yard. "Which way?" Nancy asked, keeping her voice low.

"Over there," Bess replied, pointing.

Just behind the office trailer was a familiar-looking battered blue sedan. The space on the trunk for a license plate was conspicuously empty and clean. Nancy hurried over, with Bess close behind. There were dents and scratches on the right rear fender that showed bright, unrusted metal under them. That meant they were very fresh. Nancy squatted down and examined the rear end of the car more closely.

"Aha!" she said triumphantly. With her thumb and forefinger, she plucked a fragment of greenish safety glass from the gap between the car and the bumper.

"I was right, this *is* the car!" Bess crowed.

"What are you girls doing there?" an angry voice demanded loudly. "Get away from that car!"

Nancy stood up and turned to face Al Fortunato. Kyle was right behind him. "Is this your car?" she asked.

"It's on my lot, isn't it?" he retorted. "What business is it of yours?"

123

Bess jumped in. "That car nearly hit Nancy just a few hours ago. Not long after we left here, as a matter of fact."

"Attempted homicide is very serious," Kyle added.

Fortunato scowled at him. "You're with them, are you?" he said. "I should have known. You talk pretty, but you don't know beans about carburetors."

He turned back to Nancy and said, "I can see right through your game. You think you can take up where your friend left off, do you? Well, think again. I worked hard for what I have. I'm not about to hand it over to some thieving kid on account of some cock-and-bull story about being hit by a car. You look like you're in pretty good shape to me," he added.

"Mr. Fortunato," Nancy began. "A couple of hours ago someone wearing a ski mask deliberately crashed this car into a phone booth while I was in it. I was lucky to escape without being seriously hurt."

She pointed out the fresh dents and scratches, then showed him the piece of broken safety glass. Then she said, "This *is* the car that was used, and it belongs to you. Do you care to explain, or would you rather talk to the authorities?"

Fortunato shifted uneasily and said, "I don't

know anything about hitting a phone booth, and this isn't my car, anyway."

"It's here on your lot," Kyle pointed out.

"Yeah—well, what happens is this," Fortunato replied. "Somebody's got an old junker he wants to get rid of, but since he doesn't want the hassle of transferring the title, he'll park it outside my lot and take the plates off, then walk away from it. It happens all the time. So we just drag them inside the lot and try to make a few bucks off them."

"Are you trying to tell us that this car was abandoned here this afternoon?" Bess demanded in a disbelieving tone.

"I'm not *trying* to, sweetie—I am," he replied. "And I still think you're trying to measure me for a frame. But get this, and get it right. I won't play and I won't pay. I told your buddy that, and now I'm telling you."

"Mr. Fortunato," Nancy said. "We have no intention of trying to frame you, or blackmail you, or anything else—really we don't. All we want is a few facts. Was Jack Broughton trying to extort money from you?"

Fortunato studied Nancy's face. What he saw there seemed to change his mind about her and about confiding in them. "You bet he was," he said. "I guess no one ever told him not to tangle with an old junkyard dog like me. I still got a few bites left. I told him I'd rather give the dough to my dear wife's lawyers than to him."

"I saw you downtown the night he was killed," Kyle blurted out. "You were in the coffee shop across from Mr. Drew's office."

Fortunato pulled his head down between his shoulders. He reminded Nancy of a cross between a bulldog and a turtle.

"What if I was?" he blustered. "I pay taxes in this town. I got a right to go wherever I want."

Nancy sighed to herself, then said, "Mr. Fortunato, would you mind telling me *why* you were there?"

He jammed his hands in his pockets and replied, "Since you ask so nicely, I'll tell you. Your buddy asked me for money, all right—*lots* of money. And he told me to bring it to him outside his office at six o'clock, or else. The more I thought about it, the madder I got. Finally, I made up my mind to go there and see how he liked having a few of his own teeth for dinner. But he never came downstairs. When I saw a bunch of cops show up, I decided to go on home."

"And you never went up to the office?" Nancy persisted.

"Ask him," Fortunato said, gesturing with his head toward Kyle. "He says he was there. Which reminds me—what were *you* doing there? Did Broughton try to get his hooks into you, too?"

"That's a long story," Kyle muttered, flustered.

"I think we'd better go," Nancy said. "Mr. Fortunato, thanks for your frankness. I'll come back if I have any other questions."

"Sure. Just don't expect answers unless I'm in the mood to give them," the wrecking yard owner replied. "It's not like you're the cops or anything. Sometimes I don't even answer *their* questions." He gave a deep, rumbling laugh that followed the three as they left the wrecking yard.

Outside on the street, Bess said, "I *still* think—"

"I know," Nancy said, cutting her off. "And I'm not crossing him off my list. But right now I think we have to try a different approach. It's looking more and more as though Mrs. Carlisle is at the heart of this case. How does this sound? Broughton took both copies of her will—the signed one from the vault and the one from her file—because he was hoping to extort money from her heirs."

"You mean he got them to pay him to suppress the will so that they could inherit?" Kyle asked.

"Could be," Nancy replied. "Now, if that's so, did he destroy the wills?"

"Of course not," Bess contributed. "He would

have needed to keep them. If they ever decided to stop paying, he could produce the will and the courts would take the inheritance back."

Nancy snapped her fingers. "Broughton's apartment!" she exclaimed. "When I went there, I could tell it had been searched. I figured it was the police, but maybe someone else searched it, too. Someone I interrupted by showing up like that!"

"Nancy! The one who shut you in the closet!"

"It wouldn't surprise me," Nancy said. "And if I interrupted him—"

Bess finished her sentence. "The will may still be there! Come on, guys, what are we waiting for!"

The police seal was no longer on Broughton's front door, but Nancy led her two friends around to the back, where she thought they would attract less attention. Once again, opening the back door took only seconds. She held it for Bess and Kyle, then slipped through herself.

"Nancy, what a mess!" Bess exclaimed.

Nancy turned. All the drawers and cabinet doors were hanging open. Most of their contents were in piles on the counter or the floor.

"It looks like someone paid another visit," Nancy observed. "Come on. Maybe we can find something he missed."

The living room was neater, but only because it didn't have much to mess up. The big TV and the VCR had both been turned around, as if the searcher had expected to find something hidden behind or under them. Kyle got down on the floor and ran his hand along the underside of the TV.

"When I was a kid, I used to hide letters by taping them to the bottom of my dresser," he explained. He stood up, empty-handed, and dusted off the knees of his trousers. "I guess Jack didn't know that trick."

"Let's try the bedroom," Nancy said, leading the way.

The room looked as if it had gone through a hurricane. In front of the dresser was a tangled pile of shirts, socks, and sweaters. The empty drawers had been thrown on the floor. The same fury had visited the closet.

Kyle picked up one of the suit jackets, glanced at the label, and whistled softly. "Jack had pretty expensive taste," he commented as he replaced the jacket on a wooden hanger.

Bess helped him sort through the jackets and pants. Meanwhile, Nancy studied the old rolltop desk. All the drawers and cubbyholes were emptied. There didn't seem to be much point in retracing the rifler's steps. If he had found the missing will, he had obviously taken it away with him. If he hadn't, the reason was almost certainly that the will hadn't been in the places he searched.

What about the places he might not have searched? This wasn't the first time Nancy had come across a rolltop desk. She recalled that some of them . . .

She pulled out each of the drawers in turn, feeling with her fingertips around the openings. Just when she was on the point of giving up, she felt something give slightly. She pressed harder. A small square area of the wood frame moved inward. There was a faint click, and a shallow drawer popped out of the carved molding above the opening. Inside was a folded document in a heavy paper sleeve.

"Hurray!" Nancy cried, grabbing the document. Printed on the cover, in large Old English letters, were the words *Last Will and Testament*. Winona Carlisle's name and that of Carson Drew's law firm were typed on it.

Nancy slid the will out of the sleeve and scanned the pages. Mrs. Carlisle's estate was left to several conservation organizations. There were no relatives listed as inheritors. Nancy flipped to the last page to find Mrs. Carlisle's signature and that of two witnesses.

"Let's get this back in the vault, where it belongs," she said, slipping the will back into its sleeve and putting it in her purse.

Kyle and Bess followed her out through the kitchen door. Nancy was just closing the door when there was a sudden, blinding flash of light. She spun around. Brenda Carlton was standing a few feet away with a camera aimed at Nancy and her friends.

Chapter

Fourteen

F ANTASTIC!" Brenda exulted. "Hold it right there!"

The flash went off again. Kyle jumped the steps and started toward Brenda, who hopped away, holding the camera behind her back.

"Don't you dare try anything," Brenda warned him. "I'm a reporter, and you're going to see your face on the front page tomorrow, next to my story about Carson Drew's connection to the murder of Jack Broughton."

"Now, wait a minute," Nancy said.

"What a scoop! Nancy Drew, daughter of murder suspect Carson Drew, breaks into murder victim's apartment. Was she planting evidence to clear her father? Details on page five," Brenda said.

Nancy took a deep breath and told herself to remain calm. "Brenda," she said. "If you run a story like that, you're going to end up with egg on your face. I am very close to tracking down the real killer, and as soon as I do, I promise I'll give you an exclusive—*if* you hold off with this dumb story. But if you keep hounding my father, I'll give the exclusive to Bob Broward at the *River Heights Record,* and I'll make sure your father knows exactly why the competition beat you out."

"Are you threatening me?" Brenda blustered.

"Why, no," Nancy replied sweetly. "I'm just trying to do you a favor by making sure you understand that what happens next depends on you."

Brenda stared at Nancy, then gave a quick nod. "Deal," she said. "But I'm warning you, Drew—if you're trying to string me along, you'll be sorry. Produce the goods or else!"

She turned and stalked away.

"Whew!" Bess said. "I can just imagine what my parents would say if they saw me in the paper as a burglar."

"Your parents? Huh!" Kyle added. "What about the law school admissions committee? Nancy, I sure hope you can come through on your promise."

"So do I," Nancy replied. She glanced at her watch. "Oh, no, it's late! I have to get over to the

133

library before it closes! Kyle, will you and Bess take Mrs. Carlisle's will to the office and make sure it's put back in the vault?"

"Sure," Kyle said, tucking the envelope in the inside pocket of his coat. "Should we get together later, to plan our strategy?"

"I'm supposed to meet David Megali for dinner," Nancy explained. "Bess, I'll call your house later. If you're not in, I'll leave a message on your machine. See you."

"Back issues of the *Record?*" the man at the library's reference desk said when Nancy told him what she was looking for. "Certainly. Everything more than two years old is on microfilm. You'll find them shelved downstairs, in the periodicals section. There's a copy of the index for each year down there, too. Have you used the microfilm readers before?"

"Yes, thanks," Nancy replied.

As she turned away, the librarian added, "Don't forget, we close at seven today. You'll hear a warning bell at ten to."

Nancy waved a hand in acknowledgment and headed downstairs. The dimly lit stacks in the basement were deserted. They seemed to stretch on forever. After a few minutes of searching, Nancy located the newspaper files. She pulled out several years' worth of indexes and carried them to a nearby table. It took only moments to check each one for the name Carlisle. There were at least one or two entries in most years. She copied down the dates, then swapped the indexes for another stack of them.

Finally she came to a stretch of five years with no listings for Carlisle. She stopped and scanned the notes she had made. The earliest entry was from twenty-six years earlier, and the most recent was just three years old. She decided to work backward and went to get the more recent microfilms.

Thirty minutes later Nancy sat up, discouraged, and rubbed her neck. Staring down at the screen of the reader was hard on the eyes. She had gone back over fifteen years, and she knew little more than she had when she started. About half the newspaper stories concerned various real-estate deals that Winona Carlisle had been involved in. The others were about her support for wildlife organizations. The story that got the most play was her donation, eight years earlier, of a large tract of wilderness as a nature preserve.

Nancy frowned. She was sure she had skipped over something important—something to do with the nature preserve. She found that year's microfilm again and cranked the reel to the proper date.

There it was, in the second paragraph.

The new wilderness area will be named after Mrs. Carlisle's only child, Charity, who died twelve years ago in a boating accident.

Nancy counted backward. Twelve years from the date of the donation meant twenty years ago. She went to the shelf for that year's microfilm. According to her notes, there were four Carlisle stories that year, all in July. She dried her damp palms, then began to crank the film to early July. Every instinct told her that she was on the verge of an important discovery.

The story was on page three.

Death on the River

River Heights, July 6—A family picnic ended in tragedy today when a boat carrying a local couple and their small child overturned on the Muskoka River near Sherman Park. The husband managed to carry the child to the bank, but by the time he returned to rescue his wife it was too late.

The dead woman is Charity Carlisle Megali, 26, of River Heights. Her parents . . .

Nancy straightened up so quickly that she banged her head on the hood of the microfilm reader. *Megali!* That was hardly a common last name. David must be connected to Mrs. Carlisle, which meant—

No jumping to conclusions, she reminded herself. She read each of the other stories from that tragic July. Then she sat back and chewed on the end of her pencil. Charity Carlisle had been married to a man named Jerome Megali, and their child, who was four at the time, was named David!

Not only that, there were hints that the authorities had questions about the boating accident. No one had seen it happen, but witnesses said they had heard what sounded like an angry argument just before the boat overturned. The medical examiner found that the dead woman had suffered a blow to the side of the head and had probably been unconscious when she fell into the water.

Had Jerome Megali killed his wife, with their four-year-old son as a witness, then faked the accident to hide his crime? In many ways it didn't matter. What *did* matter was that David Megali was Mrs. Carlisle's only grandchild and therefore in a direct line to inherit all her wealth —*if* she died without leaving a will that excluded him. That gave him a powerful motive to find a way to steal the will and destroy it. But how—

"Stupid!" Nancy exclaimed, slapping her forehead. She rummaged through her purse and found the envelope with Jack Broughton's résumé. She had only scanned it before, but now she looked at it more carefully. The solution to the case was right there on the first page, under Education.

"'Bachelor of Arts, Eliot College, Belleport, Washington,'" she read out loud. "So that's how David knew Jack Broughton. They were at school together!"

Suddenly Nancy froze. Had she just heard a shoe scraping on the floor somewhere nearby? She lifted her head, held her breath, and concentrated on listening. There it was again, behind her and to the left! It might be a mouse, but she didn't think so. Someone was in the basement with her—someone who didn't want her to know he was there.

Slowly, carefully, Nancy slid her chair back and started to push herself to her feet. As she did she became aware of a lemony scent—one she had smelled before in Broughton's bathroom. Now, too late to be of much help, she recalled where she had smelled it before that. It was shortly after she found Broughton's body, when David arrived at the office. She had thought she was smelling the lemon oil used to polish the furniture, but of course he must have been wearing the scent. It was just that she hadn't always noticed it.

Now she *knew* who was in the basement with

138

her, and she also knew that he didn't mean for her to leave the basement alive.

Screaming would do no good. The basement was like a tomb, silent and deep underground. No one would hear.

Nancy glanced all around without moving her head. He probably didn't know that she was aware of his presence yet. That might give her the advantage of surprise. On the other hand, he was between her and the stairway. No escape— unless she could lure him away from his position. What if she made a quick dash to the right, then doubled back to the stairway?

She took a deep breath and was ready to put her plan into motion when suddenly there was a loud click. Every light in the basement went out. Nancy was trapped in the dark by a desperate killer!

Chapter

Fifteen

HER MIND RACED. David had an advantage over her because he knew exactly where she was at the moment he turned out the lights. Her first priority was to move but not *too* quickly. Any noise she made—any collision with a table or rack of books—would reveal her new position immediately.

She strained to see in the darkness, but it was hopeless. She saw one faint gleam of light in the far distance, but nearer at hand all was blackness and gloom. With her hands out in front of her, she began to creep away from the spot where she had last heard noises.

Her fingers touched something. It was one of the metal bookshelves. But which direction was the closest end, to the left or right? She ran her hand along the shelf until she found an upright. Beyond it was a vacant space that had to be an aisle. She tiptoed in that direction and started forward again.

"Nancy!" a voice called softly. "Nancy Drew!"

She froze. Where was it coming from? Behind her? In front? The voice seemed to ricochet around the basement until it sounded as if it were coming from everywhere at once, or nowhere.

"You can't get away, Nancy," David continued, almost casually. "You know you can't. Make it easy on yourself."

She suddenly realized that the voice was moving swiftly in her direction. David must be hoping to distract her with his words while sneaking up on her.

Quickly she stepped around the shelves and into the next aisle, then flattened herself against the side. She knew David couldn't see her any better than she could see him. Breathing shallowly through her mouth, she waited.

A foot brushed the floor, so faint that she wasn't absolutely sure she heard it. It seemed to come from just behind the bookshelves. The lemony scent reached her nose again. David must be only a few feet away. She kept herself rigid and still, hoping he would pass her by and leave open the path to escape.

Another almost inaudible sound, closer this time, and a faint stirring of air. Nancy held her breath.

A hand brushed her face, then grabbed her shoulder. Nancy screamed. Quicker than thought, she bobbed her head to the left and sank her teeth into the fleshy part of the hand that grabbed her. Even before she heard the gasp and felt the pressure on her shoulder let up, she made a dash to the right, down the middle of the aisle, waving her hands in front of her to keep from crashing into a wall.

Something—a change in the reflected sound of her footsteps, perhaps—suddenly told her that there was empty space to her left. She sprang in that direction and found herself at the end of the stack. She edged around it into the next aisle and once more waited, silently gulping air. This time she was sure she had thrown David off her track.

A faint gleam of light blossomed in the aisle she had just left. Her heart sank. David had a flashlight! Any thought of evading him now was pointless. Nancy groped behind her on the shelves and grasped the tallest, thickest book she could find—in fact, it was almost as thick as the book that had killed Jack Broughton.

The light had nearly reached the end of the aisle now. Nancy carefully slid the book off the shelf and lifted it over her head in both hands.

"I know where you are, Nancy," David said, in

a voice that was almost conversational. "I see you."

He was lying. The light was still aimed forward, up his aisle.

"Why make this any harder than it has to be?" he continued, taking another step forward. "I don't want to make you suffer. I like you. That's why I let you keep on investigating for so long. But now I can't let you get in the way of my plans any longer. You understand that, don't you?"

Another step brought him into Nancy's field of view. His back was to her, but he was just a little too far away for her to risk an attack.

"You have no idea how long I've been setting my plan in motion. Fortunately, doing so was right in my line of work," he added, almost as if they were chatting over dinner.

"It was a pretty brilliant piece of investigating, you know. I had to find out who Granny Carlisle's lawyer was, then manage to infiltrate Jack into your father's firm. After that, it should have been easy. All Jack had to do was find any copies of her will and destroy them. Then he could move on, and I'd just wait for the old lady to die. But Jack got greedy. He kept the will and tried to bleed me. It didn't work, did it?

"It's such a shame that you had to walk in on me the night Jack died, Nancy," he said in the same soft voice.

"Maybe I should have taken you out of the

picture then, but I was kind. Instead, I sneaked out the door to the fire stairs and waited there." He laughed eerily. "I'm afraid you missed that, Nancy. It's around the elevator bank. Once I heard the cops come I went down to the lobby, flashed my press pass, and went back up." He paused. "You know, you wouldn't have felt a thing. It might have been kinder, but I wasn't thinking straight.

"You look like the pictures of my mother, when she was your age. Did you know that? She died when I was very little. She wanted to go away and leave me. I didn't want her to. I tried to stop her. I grabbed her by the legs, but she tripped and hit her head. And then—"

Suddenly Nancy understood the meaning of what he was saying. *That* was how David's mother had fallen, unconscious, into the river. Or at least that was what David believed. He had spent almost his whole life thinking that he had killed his own mother!

Nancy must have let out a faint sound—a gasp or a moan—because David now started to turn in her direction, swinging the flashlight toward her.

At that moment the clamor of a bell filled the library basement. Startled, David turned toward the source of the racket, and Nancy jumped out from her hiding place and brought the heavy volume down on his head. As he slumped to the floor, the flashlight flew from his hand. There was a small crash and a faint tinkle, then Nancy was once more plunged into darkness.

She edged past where she thought David must be and started in what she hoped was the direction of the stairway.

Suddenly a hand closed around her ankle.

David wasn't unconscious.

Nancy couldn't hold back. Without thinking, she raised her other foot and stamped down hard on the hand that held her ankle.

"My arm!" David screamed. "You hurt my arm!" He began to sob like a little child.

Nancy started to run, as much to get away from the sound of his crying as to escape any further attack. She had taken only a few steps when a pool of light appeared up ahead. A voice called, "Hey, who's been fiddling with the switches? What's going on down here?"

Nancy clasped her hands over her eyes as an unbearable brightness filled the basement. Then, peeping through slitted fingers, she saw a gray-haired man in a guard's uniform hurrying toward her.

"Thank goodness," she said.

Carson Drew joined Nancy at police headquarters. David Megali was at River Heights Hospital, under police guard, being treated for a broken arm and a possible concussion.

Detective Washington took the Drews to an interview room with a stenographer in a corner.

"Well, Mr. Drew," Washington began, "I owe you an apology. And I know I owe your daughter my gratitude. Without her fine detective work I don't know when this murder would have been solved."

Carson put his hand on Nancy's. "She cleared my name, too," he said, smiling at her fondly. He turned to Washington then. "You think you have a solid case against Megali?" Carson asked.

"I think we will have, once we run down a few of the leads Nancy's given us," Washington replied. "We're holding him on attempted assault now."

"I blame myself a little," Nancy's father said. "I should have been more careful about hiring Broughton. It's obvious now that Megali knew we were his grandmother's attorneys. He must have convinced his old college friend to take a job with us, specifically so he could get his hands on Mrs. Carlisle's will. From now on I intend to keep our clients' wills at the bank. That vault at the office is secure but obviously not secure enough. I thought I had checked his references, but I guess I didn't speak to the right people."

Detective Washington asked, "If I understand what you told us, Nancy, David killed Broughton because Broughton double-crossed him."

Nancy nodded. "That's right. I imagine that David went to the office that night to collect the copies of the will. When Broughton told him that he'd hidden the original, David suddenly saw himself paying blackmail to Broughton for the rest of his life. He felt his only way out was to make Broughton's life very, very short."

"That was brilliant of him to tip off the police and the press that I was stealing from my elderly clients," Carson observed. "It kept the press and the police occupied, and it gave me a good reason to want to put the blame on a burglar, which must have been his original idea."

"And meanwhile," Nancy said, "he pretended to help me with my investigation as a way of keeping tabs on me. And I fell for it. Even when he pretended to show up at Broughton's apartment and rescue me from the closet he himself had locked me in, I didn't question the coincidence. And it didn't occur to me that he had booby-trapped my car while I was waiting inside the restaurant for him. He had me completely snowed."

"Don't be so hard on yourself, Nancy. You broke the case," her father pointed out. "That's what counts."

Nancy rubbed her temples. "Yes, I guess so. The fact is, I liked him. I respected his drive to find out the truth. I have that drive myself. What

I didn't realize about David was that he was perfectly willing to suppress the truth once he'd found it out."

"He and his friend Broughton both liked to discover other people's secrets to use against them," Washington observed.

"And all his life," Nancy said, "David had been guarding the biggest secret of all—that when he was only four, he killed his own mother."

"Is that true?" Carson asked.

Washington shrugged. "We'll never know. According to the computer, Megali's father died years ago. And there weren't any other witnesses to the accident. Megali obviously *thinks* he did it, and his grandmother probably does, too. Why else would she cut her only heir out of her will?"

Nancy shook her head sadly. "I guess growing up thinking he was a killer made it easier for him to kill Broughton," she said. "And when it looked as if I was getting too close to the truth, he decided he had to kill me, too. He obviously planted that car bomb as a warning. But I think crashing into the phone booth I was in was for real."

"How did he manage to track you to the library?" Detective Washington asked.

Nancy rolled her eyes and gave a sigh of exasperation. "I guess he was following me all along," she replied. "But I made the library easy for him. I told him I was going there, and why, and when. I did everything but hand him a weapon!"

As Nancy and her father were leaving the police station, Bess and Kyle came rushing up to them.

"Nancy, are you all right?" Bess demanded. "I called your house and Hannah told me what happened."

"I've been better," Nancy said with a little laugh. "No, I'm fine. Really."

"I want to hear all about it," Bess continued. "And don't forget you promised to tell Brenda about it, too."

Nancy let out a heartfelt groan.

Kyle took Nancy's hand and shook it. "You cleared my name," he declared. "You also gave me a new aim in life."

Bess gasped. "Kyle! You mean you're not going to law school after all?"

He laughed. "Sure I am," he said. "I'm more determined than ever. But now I know that I want to go into criminal prosecution and put guys like Broughton and Megali behind bars where they belong.

"With," he added, a twinkle in his eye, "an awful lot of help from brilliant detectives like Nancy Drew!"

Nancy's next case:

Beau Winston is a hot name in fashion, and he's invited Nancy Drew into his New York studio to find out who is stealing his original designs. But now he has suffered an even greater loss—one that threatens to destroy his reputation. Someone has made off with his most prized creation: a wedding gown custom-made for heiress Joanna Rockwell.

Nancy's investigation draws her into a web of hidden motives and twisted ambitions. She uncovers a pattern of intrigue, betrayal, and revenge stretching from Manhattan's garment district to the Fifth Avenue triplex of the billionaire Rockwell family. And every new thread in the case leads to an increase in danger: for the thief of fashions is now dressed to kill . . . in *DESIGNS IN CRIME,* Case #89 in The Nancy Drew Files™.